ANYA

DENNIS W.C. WONG

CLEVERCLOCK
PRESS

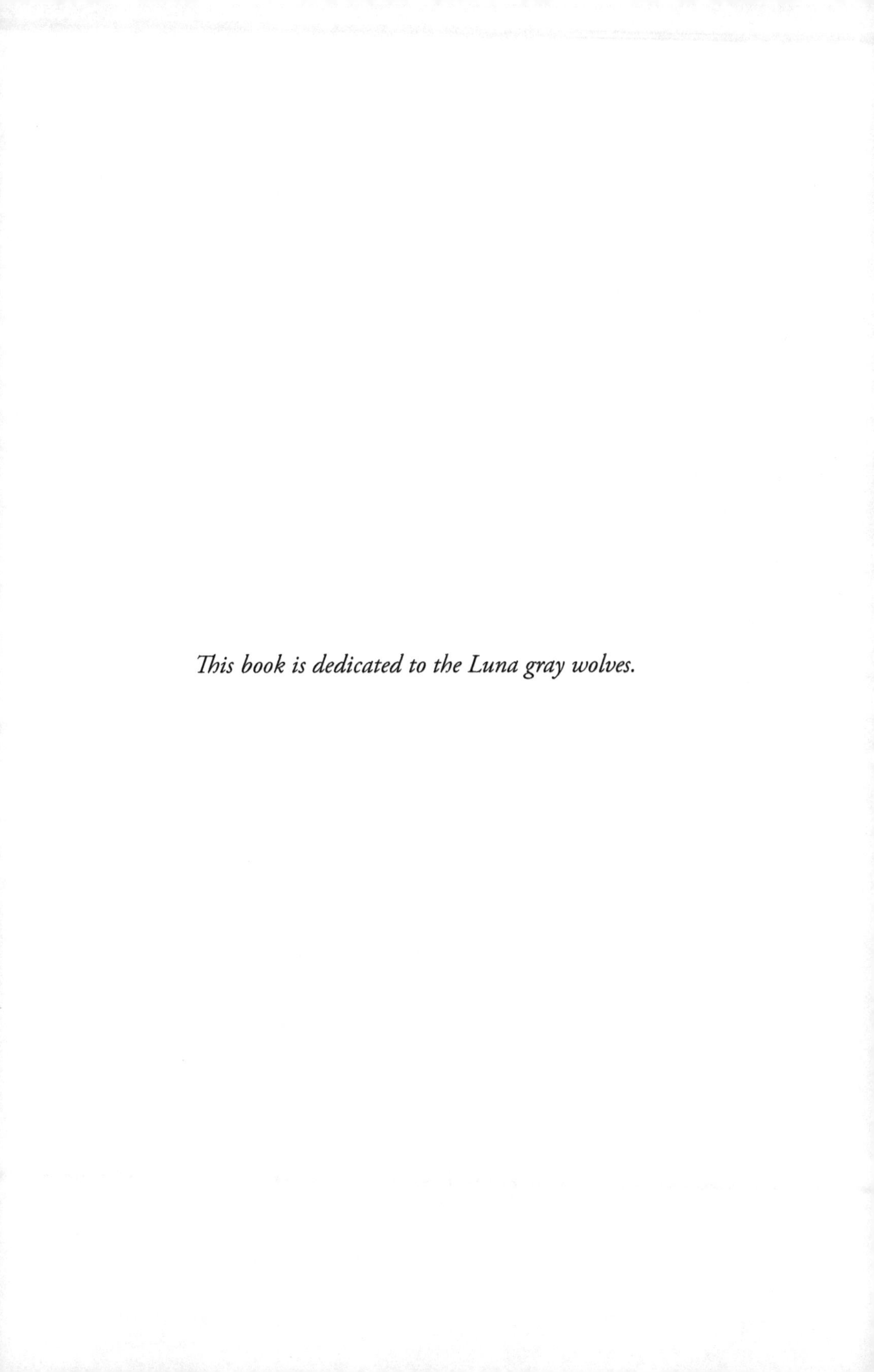

This book is dedicated to the Luna gray wolves.

Contents

Lucinda wanted people she loved to stay 1

Have you observed something? 8

While inside her room 21

Lucinda had woken up 33

When Lucinda was sure that everyone was asleep 45

We're running out of time 55

About the Author 69

LUCINDA WANTED PEOPLE SHE LOVED TO STAY

CHAPTER ONE

Lucinda wanted people she loved to stay and not leave when she got used to their presence. It had often made her sad, for to her, what was the need to get to know them when they would leave her after she had formed a close bond with them? Could her life have been fated this way, and if so, what could have been the reason for that? She had often wondered.

It had been a year since Lucinda last saw Anya. There were no dreams, communications, feelings, or voices. It felt like when Anya left; everything left with her.

"I knew I wanted her to leave at first because she was killing people, but after getting to spend days with her, I realized Anya had a beautiful soul as well. I miss her; I miss her presence; I miss everything about her help. It seemed she left with my soul." Lucinda muttered audible enough only to herself and perhaps to the immortals by her side.

"Hey! Lucinda! Is it okay to come in?" said Maya, standing at the door.

"Yeah, sure, Grandma," Lucinda said as she sat up properly.

Maya opened the door and came in. She sat down and touched Lucinda's head.

"Is everything okay? You haven't been out since morning. You know you can talk to me if you want to." Maya said, stocking her hair.

"I'm okay, just that I miss someone special, and I hope she comes back soon," Lucinda replied.

"Ever since we moved in here, I haven't seen you with anyone, so, who is the person so special that you miss?" Maya asked, popping her eyes.

"You don't know her, but when she comes back, you'll meet her," Lucinda replied. Maya considered her words in her mind but changed the topic, as her words made little sense. She took that as one of her mysterious words.

"I brought something for you," Maya said, handing a box over to Lucinda as she grabbed it and opened it immediately, eager to see what was inside. It was a beautiful bracelet.

"Thank you, but what's the bracelet for?" Lucinda asked, still holding the box of bracelets.

"Wishing you a very Happy birthday, child; it's your eighteenth birthday. I know this isn't as expensive as the necklace you have on your neck, but this is all we have for you." Maya said.

Lucinda hugged her grandmother and whispered a thank you into her ears as Maya got up and helped Lucinda put the bracelet on. Lucinda smiled and said, "I love this!"

"I'm happy you love it. Well, that's just it. I made something special for you; come and eat. You have had nothing to eat since morning." Maya said.

"Thank you, Granny, but right now I'm not hungry, but I promise to eat soon," Lucinda assured.

"Okay, no problem. Your grandpa is tending the horses; make sure you come out soon." Maya said as she stood up and left the room.

"One year already, and Anya isn't back," Lucinda said to herself and sighed as she lay back on the bed.

"Your heart is heavy; your smile is gone; sadness rules over you. You have become too withdrawn. What is bothering you, my child?" Her mom's voice sounded near Lucinda's ears, but she was startled. Lucinda had become used to ethereal voices. Whenever she heard any supernatural voice, she was no more afraid of surprise—hearing representatives from beyond the physical had become natural to her by now.

"What else but Anya. It's been one year now since she left. Ever since then, I had yearned for her presence, quested to hear her voice, but I have been met with forlorn hope. That's the reason for my sadness. I just want her to come back." Lucinda replied.

"Surely, she will come to you when it's time; I believe so, though I'm not aware when. You know, at first, you repulsed her, just like me; you were even afraid of her at a time, but suddenly you now cherish and love her. Why the sudden love for her?" Her mom asked.

"Mom, it's not just sudden. I got to spend days with Anya before she left. She might be a deadly beast, but Anya is one of the best things that can ever happen to anyone who gets to know her. I miss you and Dad, but I also miss Anya. I don't just know why life isn't fair to me. They took you and Dad away, and just when it felt I had formed a bond with someone else, she was nowhere to be found again. Why is my life this way? Why does life keep bringing people on my part when they will still leave? Why the torture? Why does it have to be this way? What did I do wrong?" Lucinda asked, wiping off the tears that were already welling in her eyes.

"You didn't wrong anyone, my child; you didn't. I don't know why it is this way, but I know you will have a reason to smile. Just believe it so." The voice replied.

"What about Dad?" Lucinda asked.

"I'm here, my dear. Happy birthday to you." Her dad's voice boomed.

"Thanks, Dad," Lucinda replied, smiling.

"Please be happy, at least for today. You still mean so much to us, and we need to see you happy." He said with tenderness in his voice.

"I will try to," Lucinda replied.

Having said so, Lucinda suddenly stood up, as if urged on by something else, feeling an urge to go out and enjoy the sun. She then walked out of her room to the sitting room, where she met her grandma.

Lucinda told her grandma she wanted to take a stroll down the road, which she obliged her, and off she went. It had been almost two months now since she ventured out of the house. Her grandma was glad that at least she wanted to go out. Lucinda had walked for about fifty meters when she heard a voice behind her.

"You look beautiful."

Lucinda turned to see who the person was, only to meet a girl about her age standing right next to her. Her hair was wooly white, and she had beautiful, starry black eyes.

"Thank you," Lucinda responded as she kept her gaze on the girl standing before her.

"I'm Star, and what's your name?"

"I'm Lucinda."

"That's nice. I live next door to that white house." Star replied.

"Oh, that sounds nice. The white house? That's where I live." Lucinda replied.

"That means we are neighbors. Great! I hope to see you more often." Star said and bade her goodbye without waiting for further conversation with her.

Lucinda smiled as she kept strolling down the road. She was looking around, hoping to see the little girl, Amber, but she had no success in that. Lucinda did not also know where to look for her. Having spent close to one hour outside, she went back home.

When she got back to their house, she walked straight to the kitchen and opened the plate close to the pot where her food was kept. She took the spoon and started eating the food while sitting down on a chair in the kitchen. Half through her meal, she became full. She covered the plate and left the kitchen, back to her room.

As soon as she lay on the bed, she remembered the girl next door she had just met outside about an hour before. She was surprised to know that such a girl lived next door to them, wondering why she hadn't met her ever since they came to live in the city. Finding the thought irritating, she waved it away and soon was fast asleep. However, she just had one name on her lips, Anya.

****

Three days later, Lucinda was out again, and it seemed as if Star was found everywhere Lucinda was, or instead, it was Star's silhouette. Lucinda was startled as she increased her pace, but Star kept coming closer. Finally, she had to give up and accept Star around herself. Star looked nice as a young girl at their first meeting yesterday, but it seemed something was off about her. Lucinda promised herself to find out what it was.

As Lucinda couldn't take it anymore, she returned home. So she walked into the garden and sat down. Shortly after, she started hearing some noises, and on turning to the direction the noises were coming from, she saw Star coming into the garden.

"How did you find out I'm here?" Lucinda asked.

"Oh, I normally see you through my window. I saw your grandparents when they were leaving." Star replied.

"Yes, they went out to get a few things that we need here in the house," Lucinda replied.

"That's nice," Star replied, smiling.

"So why are you here?" Lucinda asked.

"Well, I was just bored at home, and I needed someone to talk to," Star replied.

"I have never seen your parents; where are they, or don't they leave the house at all?" Lucinda asked.

"Sadly, I lost my parents a few years ago, and I'm the only one that lives in the apartment. It's so sad, but I miss them. I have been alone ever since they died. I saw when you moved in last year, but I feared getting to know you because I felt you might be the harsh, snobby type, as you were always indoors." Star replied.

"I'm not harsh; neither am I unfriendly, but I just like being on my own. But, first, let me say you're the first human friend that I have ever had since I was born." Lucinda replied.

"What do you mean by 'First human friend'?" Star asked.

"Nothing," Lucinda replied and stared into thin air.

"Something is bothering you; you don't look happy," Star asked.

"I just miss my parents. It's been a long time since I saw their faces, and I would do anything to see them again." Lucinda replied.

"Where are they?" Star asked.

"They are dead; they died when I turned ten. Memories of that day are still fresh in my mind. It has been eight whole years without them. The journey hasn't been easy." Lucinda replied as she quickly wiped off the tears trickling down her cheeks.

"I'm so sorry about your parents," Star said.

"Thank you," Lucinda replied.

"So, who are you? Tell me more about yourself." Lucinda asked.

"I need to get going. Your grandparents might be back soon, and I'm not sure they would want to meet me here," Star said as she quickly stood up and walked away.

"Strange," Lucinda muttered, got up, and wanted to go into the house before changing her mind. She had the urge to speak to her parents about Star.

"Mom, Dad, it's been three whole days, and I haven't heard from you. What's happening? If I have annoyed you both, I'm sorry. Have you left too? Even if you both were leaving, you would have told me, but could it be you left without a notice? I already miss your voices." Lucinda was saying to herself.

Ever since she first met Star three days ago, Lucinda had heard from her parents. She was dying to tell them about the girl next door who seemed strange and would always be elusive anytime she asked her questions about herself.

Lucinda was still in the garden when Maya walked in to inform her they were back from the market.

"I got this for you," Maya said, handing some apples to Lucinda.

"Thanks, Granny," Lucinda replied, smiling.

"You're welcome, my darling," Maya said as she left her and walked inside the house, smiling.

Lucinda knew she had all the love she needed, but she wanted more. Was she selfish? No. She was just questing for what every child out there would ask for; their parents' love. She ruminated over these as she chewed her apples.

"How I wish I could see my parents' face again, even if was to be for a second one last time. They were in pain before they died; it hurts so much." She said as she stood up and walked into the house to assist her grandmother.

As the days rolled by, Lucinda became more outgoing, meeting with Star often and feeling happier. Maya and Greg were elated that Lucinda wasn't always locked inside like before. But Lucinda kept wondering about the person of her new friend, Star. Though Star made her happy with her grandparents, there was this strange aura around her she couldn't place her fingers on, and she kept evading Lucinda's questions about who she was, but that didn't deter Lucinda from asking. She was a very demanding girl. She was determined to find out who Star was.

Star never visited whenever Greg and Maya were at home. Instead, she would visit when they were out. Occasionally, Lucinda had wanted to know from her why she had never visited anytime her grandparents were around. Still, she gave silly excuses, which gave her room for more significant doubt about who Star was.

"I must find out who you're; and what you want," Lucinda said that night as she lay on her bed before she drifted off to bed.

HAVE YOU OBSERVED SOMETHING?

CHAPTER TWO

"Have you observed something?" Maya asked Greg, who was engrossed in the book that he was reading.

"What's that?" Greg asked, with his eyes still fixed on the book.

"Lucinda is not always at home these days, and I don't know who she goes out to meet. So I'm getting worried." Maya asked.

"Lucinda is eighteen, and she can take care of herself. I observed that too, but I just kept shut; at least she is no longer stuck in her room." Greg replied.

"It's okay for her to make friends; that has been our prayers, but we need to know who her friend is," Maya replied

Just then, Lucinda walked in with smiles on her face as she greeted her grandparents.

"Lucinda, can you please have a seat? Your grandpa and I want to have a word with you?" Maya said.

"Sure," Lucinda replied as she sat down close to her grandpa.

"We observed that you have been leaving the house every day, which explains that you now have a new friend. Don't you think it's okay for us to see her?" Greg replied.

"We're not saying it's wrong for you to have a friend; we are just watching out for you. We are more than happy that you no longer curl up in your room all alone, but at least we would love to see her; maybe invite her over for lunch." Maya replied.

"Oh, you mean Star; she is the only friend I have," Lucinda replied.

"So, where does she live?" Maya asked.

"So, you haven't seen Star? The girl with white hair and dark eyes? Her skin is white." Lucinda replied.

"No, we have not," Greg replied.

"But she always sees you guys when you both are going out. So anyway, just like I said earlier, her name is Star, and she lives next door." Lucinda replied.

"You're joking, right?" Greg asked.

"No, I'm not," Lucinda replied, laughing.

"You have got to be kidding. You're not serious." Maya added.

"Why? What's wrong? I don't understand you both." Lucinda replied.

"That's because there is no one living next door," Maya replied.

"I don't understand. What do you mean by there is no one next door?" Lucinda asked, perplexed.

"No one lives in that house; it's been over a decade now since the last occupant. The man who sold this house to me told me the occupants of that building, the man and his wife, slept and never woke up. So that house has been empty, even before we moved in." Greg replied.

"That's not true; Star always sees you both anytime you and Grandma are leaving together. I have seen her come out of the house countless times." Lucinda replied.

"Have you ever entered inside that house before?" Maya asked.

"No, I've not. We always talk outside or take a stroll together." Lucinda replied.

"That explains it all; your said friend isn't human, most probably. Star isn't human, most likely. No one lives in that house." Maya replied.

"This whole thing is still not making sense. I will be in my room." Lucinda said as she abruptly left her grandparents and walked into her room.

"This is serious. She has seen a ghost." Maya said.

"I won't say it's a ghost; maybe someone different who lied that she is living next door," Greg replied.

"I just hope what you said is true," Maya replied as she stood up and walked into the kitchen.

Lucinda sat on her bed as she looked around her room. She became a bit terrified at the possibility of Maya's words.

"Who the hell are you, Star?" Where did you come from?" Lucinda muttered.

Her grandma was right. She started soliloquizing. Most probably, Star isn't human, after all. No wonder she never let me into the apartment; no wonder anytime a question is thrown at her about herself, she deflects it. If Star isn't human, then who is she? Why did she come to me? What business does she have with me? Who is she? she concluded as she stood up and when to the sitting room.

"Tell me more about the occupants of the house next door that died," Lucinda said, sitting close to her grandpa.

"The man only told me that after their baby girl disappeared, the next day they died," Greg replied.

"Like how old was the little girl, and what's her name?" Lucinda asked.

"The girl was just ten years old then, and she should be twenty by now since it's over a decade it happened. Well, no one knew their child's name because no one saw the child. But what people knew was that day the man and his wife said they were looking for their child; and that she was ten years old, and then the next day, they died in their house. Since then, the house has been vacant." Greg replied,

"Do you know the name of the man and his wife?" Lucinda asked.

"Why you are asking all these questions, Lucinda? We weren't here when the whole thing happened. Well, I don't know their names, but the man said the occupants of the house were magicians, but you won't know because they kept it hidden." Greg replied.

"Then how did your informant know since the man had kept it a secret?" Lucinda asked.

"The man was his brother; he sold the house to me because he couldn't afford to stay in this city anymore. He wouldn't enjoy staying in this case because staying here would keep reminding him of his brother. As for the child he had, he never got to see her." Greg replied.

"Something doesn't seem right," Lucinda whispered.

"What do you mean?" Greg asked.

"The girl child they claimed disappeared might be Star because Star mentioned her parents died when she was still little," Lucinda replied.

"Star, or whatever you said her name is, isn't the man's child. Listen, Lucinda, I have always known you to differ from the rest of the world, but whosoever Star is, she is trouble; avoid her." Greg replied.

"That's not a problem. Right now, you and Grandma are the only friends I have. Star's chapter has been closed." Lucinda replied.

"What are you up to?" Greg asked.

"Nothing, I'm not doing anything. Why did you ask?" Lucinda asked as she smiled.

"It's easy to see that your smile isn't genuine. The Lucinda I know will never agree to something without a fight, and you just agreed to something without quarreling over it just now." Greg replied.

"That's because I'm growing. Lucinda is getting older. I'm maturing. I'm eighteen, Grandpa. Let me remind you if you had forgotten." Lucinda replied.

"I haven't," Greg replied, smiling.

"Where is Grandma?" Lucinda asked.

"In the kitchen," Greg replied.

"Okay, let me check up on the horses," Lucinda said as she stood up and walked outside.

When Lucinda got to the stable, she walked in and went straight to the horses. She fed the horses with hay cubes and replaced their drinking water, and when she was done, she closed the stable and made it towards the balcony. As soon as Lucinda sat down, she remembered she had not found Amber. She immediately got up and walked outside, yelling: "Grandpa, I'm coming," and off she went down the street.

"I need to find her. Maybe I can get to ask her some questions," Lucinda muttered under her breath as she went to the spot where she had seen her months back, but she couldn't find her. She then stopped passersby and described Amber, but no one knew her. The day was losing its sun already when Lucinda gave up as she turned and journeyed back home.

On her way going home, Lucinda stopped by the oak tree that was close to their building, as she rested a little and took fresh air under the branches of the tree, for it had been so long since she did that. She sat down on the ground and leaned against the trunk of the oak tree, closing her eyes and breathing in deeply.

"Have you been looking for me?" As Lucinda opened up her eyes to see Amber standing right in front of her, a voice said.

"Amber, how did you know I was looking for you? I had searched everywhere, but I couldn't find you. I even asked people around about you,   but nobody seemed to know who you are," Lucinda replied excitedly.

"Well, I didn't want you to meet you where ordinary eyes would see us. I knew you were going to rest on the oak tree, so I had to wait for you here." Amber said as she sat close to Lucinda.

"Is your name Amber?" Lucinda asked.

"If you don't like it, you can still call me something else," Amber replied.

"No, I don't mean that. You have a nice name." Lucinda replied.

"You're looking for me because Anya asked you to find me by all means because I'm going to be of help to you when the time comes. Guess you came a little late; you didn't make a move all this while. You were embittered about Anya's disappearance. I know you miss her, but if you had searched for me immediately after Anya left, maybe you would have easily found out who Star is before now." Amber said.

"You know her? What do you know about her? I need to know, please." Lucinda pleaded.

"All the answers you seek are in the Book of Prophecy; it holds every story you need to know; prophecies that were given even before your birth," Amber replied.

"What prophecies are you talking about? How does it link with me? Right now, the only thing I need to know is all about Star. I need answers on who she is and what she wants from me." Lucinda replied.

"Just like I said earlier, all the answers you seek are in the Book of Prophecies. So, when you get hold of it, you will know who Star is. I would love to tell you, but the truth is I can't, Lucinda. And yes, all the prophecies are linked to you because you're the daughter of the Moon and the Stars." Amber replied.

"I never wanted this life." Lucinda protested as she picked a pebble and threw it in the air.

"This Life chooses you. Of course, there are obstacles on the way, but time will come when you have to choose, and it will be the hardest task ever. But I trust you will make the right decision." Amber replied as she left.

"You're leaving already. I still need answers. I understand it's late, and your people might look for you; how do I find you again?" Lucinda replied.

"By this oak tree; when you get here, I will notice because you have a strong connection that leads people to you. That was why Star could find you so quickly." Amber replied.

"You're a child, but you're not a child," Lucinda replied.

"I'm the seer who has reincarnated for four times now. I was here when you were like the other queen and was killed, but I never got to see her face. The same queen is you. You're back again; just that it took you long to come back to Earth. So, I kept reincarnating, hoping that I would someday be opportune to see the queen, and here I am today, standing right next to her." Amber said, smiling.

"Before you go: The Book of Prophecy; how do I get it?" Lucinda asked.

"It is on your own, for what you seek is closer to you. You need to hurry back home. Your grandparents are already worried that you're not yet back. So go home, Lucinda. We will meet some other time." Amber said as she raced off.

Lucinda got up and went back home. Immediately, she pushed the door open and walked inside. Maya threw the first question at her.

"Where are you coming from?" Maya asked.

"Just went a strolling. I need to wrap my head around what you both told me about the apartment next door." Lucinda replied as she went straight to her room and lay on the bed.

"Star: who is she, and what does she want from me?" Lucinda asked herself.

Mom, Dad, where are you both? I need you both now. I haven't heard from any of you for a long time now, and it's making me get worried. Even if you people wanted to leave, you would have said goodbye. Please, I need you both to say something to me. I just want to hear your voice." Lucinda pleaded.

After not hearing any voice, Lucinda removed her necklace and held it in her hands. Next, she brought out the Seashell and placed both of them on the bed, but she returned the Seashell after some hesitations.

Lucinda held the necklace as she looked at it as tears trickled down her cheeks.

"The one who gave me the necklace isn't around anymore, and it's heartbreaking. Anya left, and she left with everything. And now I can't even hear from my parents anymore. Life has always been unfair to me; Life has taken people whom I love and care about. They rarely get to stay with me. I hope that one day I will have a reason to put this necklace on confidently." Lucinda placed the necklace in the same box with the Seashell as she closed it and hid it under her bed.

She lay on the bed, staring at the ceiling before sighing: "This isn't the life I had wanted, but here I am living it."

****

"Do you think Lucinda is telling the truth about the girl in the next building?" Maya asked.

"Of course, Lucinda wouldn't have come up with fabricated stories. Maybe she might have met the said girl couple of times, and maybe the girl might have lied to her. She lives in the apartment next to ours." Greg said.

"But how come we haven't seen this girl before? Is she a ghost?" Maya asked.

"The girl has her reasons; she made herself known to Lucinda only, and I don't know why," Greg replied.

"What if someone lives there and we don't know?" Maya asked.

"Maya, the apartment has had no occupants for years now, and I believe whoever the girl is, she isn't coming back again," Greg replied.

Lucinda woke up the following day and went about with her routine chores. When she was done, she told her grandparents she was going out. She didn't wait to get their permission as she jogged off.

Soon she got to the oak tree and sat on the ground, just like she did yesterday, leaning on the trunk.

"Why did you take off your necklace?" Then, as Lucinda turned back to see Amber leaning on the tree by her side, the voice said.

"When did you get here? How come I didn't notice, and how did you know I was here?" Lucinda asked.

"I got here even before you told your grandparents you were going out. So I knew you were coming. But, again, you are the daughter of the Moon and the Stars; and it wouldn't be wise to keep you waiting." Amber replied.

"Thank you for coming." Lucinda simply said.

"You came here to ask me questions. The answers which you seek are just close to you, and it will show itself." Amber replied.

"My parents; I haven't heard their voice for a very long time. I need to know why. Even if they were leaving, at least they should have said goodbye. I need to know what's wrong." Lucinda asked.

Amber stared at Lucinda and blurted out: "The time is fast approaching when you have to choose between your parents and humanity.

"What do you mean?" Lucinda asked

"You still haven't answered my question; why did you take off your necklace?" Amber asked.

"It reminds me so much about Anya. I miss her, but sadly, it's like I can't see her ever again. She left without a goodbye, and when she left, she left with everything; no dreams, no visits from people from the world beyond. Everything just went with her." She paused before continuing almost immediately, "Life has never been fair to me; first, they took my parents and now they took Anya and just this little grace of me hearing my parent's voice, I don't know what happened to it; and suddenly, they are mute. So, what's the use of wearing the necklace when the person who gave me the necklace is no more? I can't see her; I can't hear her voice. So, I had to remove it because it reminds me so much about Anya, as simple as that," Lucinda replied.

"I understand your pain, but all these are tests. You don't need to worry about Anya because when you need her, she will return." Amber replied.

"Really? Lucinda became excited, which didn't last long before being replaced by melancholy again. "I need her now. I have always missed her presence ever since she left." Lucinda replied.

"You don't need her now. When you do, she will find her way back to you." Amber replied.

"What about my parents? What do you mean; time is fast approaching when I have to choose between them and humanity? My parents are already dead, and I have found consolation in their voice so, why should I choose between them and humanity?" Lucinda asked, trying hard not to break down.

"I understand you, and I feel your pain, but the Prophecy was written years before you were born, and it has to be that way; no one can change it," Amber replied.

"All this isn't fair; all these that are happening. I am the daughter of the Moon and the Stars. As everyone claimed, why is my life so difficult? Why do I always lose people just when I have formed a bond with them? Today I'm with you now, but I won't be surprised if they also take you away by tomorrow. Any of those manipulating my life has never valued my happiness. My life is incomplete shambles; everything is ruined. I just want to live like every other girl out there in the world, but no, you all have made life so miserable for a little girl like me." Lucinda replied as she stood up.

"Being a leader comes with so many responsibilities, Lucinda. You just have to understand that." Amber said.

"A task which includes taking loved ones away? That's not possible. I'm fed up; I'm tired of this life I'm living. Maybe one day, you all won't have anyone to call the daughter of the Moon and the Stars because I will definitely find a way to end all of these, and even if I don't find a way, I will end this miserable life." Lucinda replied.

"You will not try that," Amber replied.

"Of course, I will. I'm completely fed up, and if at all you are worried about what will happen to my grandparents, that's not an issue as I'm ending my life together with theirs. That way, I will be at peace." Lucinda replied.

"You're angry and..." Amber was about to say.

"Yes, I'm angry; I'm angry about my parent's death; I'm angry that just this means of communicating with them has been stopped. I'm angry about Anya. I'm angry with the way my life is. I'm angry that I became friends with this girl next door, only to find out she isn't real. Maybe she is a ghost that I don't know of. I'm angry about everything; I am angry, and the only thing I'm thinking of now is how to end it all," Lucinda replied.

"This too shall pass; you just need to be strong. These are just mere challenges that will pass away." Amber replied.

"Challenges, you say? I'm tired. I don't want to be involved in any of these anymore." Lucinda replied as she turned to leave, but she stopped as she turned back and said, "And even if I was to choose between saving humanity and my parents, I would choose my parents ten times over."

Lucinda turned and walked back home. She needed to clear her head. When Lucinda got home, she went straight for the stable; and took the white horse as she mounted it, whispering into the horse's ear before they galloped away. She was going back to their village, her parents' village.

When she got there, she went straight to the riverbank, and sitting down; she started throwing pebbles into the river.

"Surely, this isn't the life I wanted. This isn't how I thought my life was going to be. Everything is changing, and they expect me to move with every crazy change. No way. I became friends with this girl next building, and after forming a bond with her, I found she were fake to me. Look at my parents; look at Anya; look at my grandparents. No, I have never had a cheerful story to say about my life. Things might have started nicely, but now everything will end in ruins. I don't want to be called the daughter of the Moon and the Stars anymore; I don't want to be the Earth Goddess again. Both are useless; they are just useless since I can't even know or see beyond what I'm permitted to see and know. It's simply frustrating. I never wanted this life.

I just want to be like every other young girl out there, but my case is the opposite. I'm tired; I'm tired of being unhappy; tired of losing loved ones, and right now, the only thing I can think of is how to end this miserable life. I have always been termed strong by grandparents, but the truth is, this Lucinda here is getting weaker and weaker every day.

I just want to experience lifelong happiness like others. I don't want my life to be filled with challenges, and I don't want people I love leaving me." She paused and threw some pebbles into the water before continuing.

"Goddess of this water, I don't know if you can hear me; I need your help; I need someone to help me and end all this else because I might wake up one morning and end it all myself. So maybe you can't hear me, but you all were quick to come during Anya's time with me, and now you're all quiet." Lucinda said as tears dripped down her cheeks.

"Free me, let me go! Release me! I'm tired! I don't want to be the daughter of the Moon anymore!" Lucinda shouted, holding her head as she shrieked the more.

"This isn't the life I wanted. Maybe it's the life my mom wanted, but you all should have waited for me to grow older and ask for my permission first. My mom made a simple request; she was just a poor, naïve woman who wanted to give everything to her child. She was merely dreaming, never knowing that her request could be granted.

I'm hundred percent sure that she wouldn't want me to be in this mess today. It was just a harmless wish. Now, I'm sure you were the ones that took my parents away.

You were the ones that made it possible for me to hear them. I am consoled with just hearing their voices, yet suddenly you also made that cease. Just tell me, why I won't tire of this life. Anya came, and suddenly she was nowhere to be seen. Why is that so? And now the first friend I ever had, I woke up only to wake up one morning to discover that she wasn't real, or should I say, she was just a figment of my imagination.

Tell me, why I won't be angry. Why won't I be tired of the recent happenings in my life? I'm fed up, and I want to live like any other girl out there, but you all make things difficult for me. I do not wish to be one of you if I had ever been. Take title you gave to me. This young girl here is tired, and she wants to go. You all have to end it; else, I will end it myself.

How does it make sense that I will have to choose between my parents and humanity? What sort of hard choice is that? I will choose my parents ten times over. Please, please, please; I wasn't aware when this whole thing started. Please, just take it back. Free me; I'm tired!" Lucinda shouted as she covered her face with her two palms, as she started saying in between sobs.

"Lucinda does not want to be involved with this anymore. She isn't that strong anymore. This Lucinda is tiring of all the drama that has been happening in her life, and right now, the only thing she needs is her peace." She bent down and hid her head in between her legs.

But after a long while, she stood up and went straight to where she tethered her horse, untied it, mounted it while saying, "I remember when my mom was in this body; and now I can't hear from her anymore. This life is so cruel, and I have done nothing to deserve it." And having said this, she galloped away.

WHILE INSIDE HER ROOM

CHAPTER THREE

While inside her room, Lucinda was busy arranging her clothes. She had been indoors for three straight days without venturing out. She had been melancholic again, sitting all day, mourning her parents and her loss of Anya.

"Did you miss me?" A voice said as Lucinda turned to see Star right inside her room.

"The last time I checked, my room was locked. So how did you get in?" Lucinda asked. She was still busy with her clothes but casting a furtive glance at Star.

"Because I'm Star; I can do anything I want," said Star.

"Really? I thought you were the girl from the next apartment. Do girls from the next building appear and disappear at will? How did you get into my room? Who are you, and what do you want because it's obvious you have lied to me all these times?" Lucinda replied as she finally sat on her bed, clutching some clothes in her hands.

"Star, that's the name," Star replied, smiling.

"Please sparc me. I already know your name—Star, the girl who lied to me so that she could come close to me. I have no time. What do you want?" Lucinda asked, clearly infuriated.

"You have been here crying like a baby because you haven't heard your parents' voice for months now. Well, I caged their spirit; at least that's the only powers I have left, and I used it wisely. So if you want your parents to talk to you again, I just need you to uncage my body. I need to be free; I want to return to Earth." Star replied.

"Is that all?" Lucinda asked.

"Yes, I knew you would comply; it's very easy, the only…"

"Just keep shut, Star." Lucinda bellowed.

"You appeared in my room from God knows where and you are here to tell me what to do and what not to do. You dare to cage my parents and for months. I haven't heard their voice, and now you're here to blackmail me. Dream on. Do you think you can walk in here and tell me what to do?

Do you think you can make me do things against my wishes? You must be joking. Though you have caged my parents, I just need to make you understand it won't make me free your body or whatever you're talking about. Rather, I'll find a way to end your life forever and make you cease to exist in this world for daring to deceive and blackmail me." Lucinda thundered.

"You will never hear from your parents again." Star calmly said.

"I'm Lucinda. That's the name my mom gave to me. I am the daughter of the Moon and the Stars even before I was born into this Earth. I do things my way, and if you think you can threaten me by using my parents, then it's a failed mission. My parents will come back, when I need them! You're such a pathetic loser." Lucinda replied.

"I know how close you're to your parents. You think about them every day; you would run back to me to do my biddings. It's just a matter of time." Star replied.

"I guess you have to wait forever because your wish will never be granted," Lucinda replied.

"Then we shall see," Star replied and disappeared.

Lucinda sighed as she continued with arranging her clothes. When she was done, she placed them carefully in her wardrobe as she went back to her bed and lay down. She stared at the ceiling as memories of the time she spent with her parents started playing in her mind. Star was right; her parents were everything to her though they were dead. But that which Star wanted would never happen. So, she would look for other means to bring her parents back.

"Star went too far by caging my parents. She knew what was going to hurt me. That's why she did what she did. But I will not set her free. Rather, I will find a way to set my parents free. I didn't enjoy enough time with my parents when they were alive, and now that they are no more, they won't still allow me to enjoy their voices. Fate is trying so hard to break me down, knowing very well that my parents are my source of hope and strength.

They have done nothing to deserve what has come to them. And as for Star, she has hit me with a stone today; and I'm already so hurt and bleeding. During my time here, I will end her life. If my parents can die when they have done nothing wrong, then people like Star don't deserve to live both spirit and body," Lucinda said as she stood up and walked out of the room.

"Where are you going to?" Greg asked as he noticed Lucinda was leaving the house.

"I just want to take a stroll," Lucinda replied.

"Are you telling me the truth, or you're just trying to deflate my question? Where exactly are you going to?" Greg asked.

"I just need to meet up with someone, but for the records, the person isn't Star. I'm going out to meet a kid I met in the market, whom I enjoy being with." Lucinda replied.

"What's her name?" Greg asked.

"Amber, that's her name," Lucinda replied

"Reminds me of the great seer; her name was Amber too. I had wanted to meet her when she was alive, but I guess I was late; she died. That was years back." Greg replied.

Lucinda turned and sat close to her grandpa, suddenly animated. "Tell me more about this seer," Lucinda asked, with her eyes flashing excitingly.

"I thought you're going out?" Greg asked.

"That can wait, but at least tell me who the seer was," Lucinda asked.

"Amber was her name. She was so beautiful. That's what many who saw her said. She never got old; she was always young though she had lived for many years. She sees everything the ordinary eyes can't see.

She can predict what will happen in the future; she is powerful. People who visited her said she was always sad because she hadn't met the daughter of the Moon and the Stars. No one knew who the daughter of the Moon and the Stars was. But one thing was certain; if you meet Amber the seer, she was would always proffer a solution to your problems. And one day, she died in her sleep. I was hurt because I made plans to see her after you were born. I wanted to ask questions about the birthmark you had." Greg replied.

"My birthmark? Why did you say so?" Lucinda replied.

"Because I saw the birthmark changes in it's position in the mid-night with full moon, I was with you there! I was dumbfounded; I wanted to tell your mother, but I knew she would not believe me, and that was when I said I was going to meet Amber, the great seer, hoping she would have answers to my questions. Still, unfortunately, on my arrival at her place, I was told she died the night before," Greg replied.

"Strange," Lucinda said, folding her hands.

"That was when I knew something was off. You were a special child, but I needed more explanations. Sadly, I didn't get that. So, I lived with that all my life. I didn't tell anyone because no one would ever believe me. But I'm happy you have grown to be the sweetest soul on Earth. Though your parents might have left early, I knew you were strong; and that someday life is going to return all that they took from you." Greg replied.

"I hope so; I hope life returns to everything. I will be patiently waiting for that day. The darkness has stayed way too long, and it took so many things away. Right now, I only wish for the light to come because I know it's bringing all the things I lost." Lucinda replied.

"Do you care for a hug?" Greg asked.

"Sure, Grandpa," Lucinda said as she wrapped her hands around her Grandpa's body.

"See you later. I promise to be home soon." Lucinda replied as she stood up and left the house.

When Lucinda got to the oak tree, she sat down and waited patiently for Amber. Thirty minutes was already gone, but there was no sight of Amber. Lucinda stood up, feeling dejected as she walked away, when a voice called her back. She turned to see Amber running towards the oak tree.

"Grandma wouldn't let me, so I had to sneak out. Sorry that I kept you waiting." Amber said as soon as she got to where Lucinda was standing. She was panting.

"She came; she is the real reason I haven't heard from my parents for a long time," Lucinda replied.

"Yes, she is! Star wants you to free her body. Only then will she free your parents. Her spirit is just wandering here on Earth, and the only power she had was what she used to in caging your parents. So, tell me, will you set her free?" Amber asked.

"I won't set her free, never! She should have known by now that no one tells Lucinda what to do. I do things my way, and she made the worst mistake when she picked my parents and caged their voices. She made the worst mistake ever.

So, I will not set her free. Rather, I'm going to destroy her. And about my parents, I will find a way to set them free. Star might have her powers, but I'm hundred percent sure that she isn't stronger than me. She messed with the wrong person." Lucinda replied.

"I don't know where this courage came from, but I like the new Lucinda," Amber replied.

"She knows how much I loved my parents. She knows my parents were everything to me. She knows I draw strength from the voice of my parents, and she caged their voice, and she came back to give me conditions. One thing is certain, and Star isn't human. Sure. Who is she then?" Lucinda asked.

"You are close to solving the puzzle. You have realized that Star isn't human. I'm glad you realized that quick." Amber asked.

"My grandpa mentioned the name…"

"Amber the seer," Amber said, cutting Lucinda short.

"How did you know?" Lucinda asked.

"How wouldn't I know? I am she. Yes, when he wanted to meet me. I was already dead by the time he came, but I'm back now. You won't understand, Lucinda, so it's of no use explaining to you.

When I was born again a few years back, the woman who bore me died at childbirth, and people who came to see me said I look like Amber, the seer that died many years ago; and that's why I was named Amber, but I am that Amber that died many years ago. I'm back to life. I came back just to see you, and I'm glad I have been opportune to see you. Now back to why we are here; you're here because you want to know who Star is and to ask questions about the birthmark based on what your grandpa told you.

Yes, the Stars and the Moon changed their position on your body, but what your grandpa failed to notice was that one Star was missing, and that was the day the people from the other world acknowledged your birth.

Four Stars are still on your back, which shows you can still come back to this Earth four times. Each time you come back, one Star will miss until all disappears, and when that time comes, another will be chosen to be the daughter of the Moon and the Stars." She stopped talking and was observing Lucinda with teary eyes.

"Your heart is heavy, and you're in pain. Star has touched you where she shouldn't, and you want nothing but revenge. The last time we met, I told you a time would come when choosing between your parents and saving humanity.

Life has taken so many things from you; darkness is hovering around, but once Star is dealt with and cleared from the picture, the light will come back, and it's going to bring all that has been taken from you. Believe me," Amber said.

"That was the exact words my grandpa used just some minutes ago before I left the house, but do you think all that was taken from me? Do you think they will ever be returned?" Lucinda asked.

"By that, you mean your parents? Just remember, life will return to whatever was taken from you. You don't have to know how." Amber said.

"How do I stop Star? I need help." Lucinda asked.

"Hmmm. Well, I can't help you with that. It's left for you to figure that out on your own. You can only fight the battle. And even if you need help, Anya is the only one who can help you out, not me," Amber replied.

"Hmmm. It's already a year since Anya left, and I don't know when she will return. How can she be the only one to help me out of this situation when I haven't seen her or even seen her in my dreams? Though you said Anya would come again, that is left to be believed. I'm not sure she will come back." Lucinda replied.

"Don't be so sure," Amber replied.

"I'm sure," Lucinda replied.

"Have you forgotten she told you she would come when you need her? Anya always keeps to her words. The only truth here is that you don't need Anya now. When you do, she will come; and she will run back to you." Amber said.

"What does Star want from me? I need to know." Lucinda replied.

"I might be a seer, but there are things I do not know; things that are meant for the eyes and ears of the daughter of the Moon and the Stars, but one thing I'm sure of is that the answers you seek are just closer to you.

The answers you seek are in the Book of Prophecy, the only book which has been locked for centuries, and you're the only one who has the key to it.

Find it, and there you will know who Star is and what she wants from you and how you can destroy her because if you set Star free, doom and chaos shall reign upon Earth; and you won't be spared, either." Amber said and ran off. She didn't wait to listen to Lucinda speak.

"Gone! She didn't even wait to answer me or to direct me. The Book of Prophecy? Where do I even look for it? I do not know how to get the book and talk about the key. I don't have the key to anything. This is going to be a bigger hard nut to crack." Lucinda said as she sighed and started on her way back home.

"So, did you meet her?" Greg asked as soon as he saw Lucinda step into the house.

"Yes, I did, and I'm home. Where is Grandma?" Lucinda asked.

"She is taking a nap," Greg replied.

"Can I ask you something? Don't freak out, please." Lucinda pleaded.

"Sure, what's the question?" Greg asked, dropping his glass of coffee.

"What do you know, or is there anything like the Book of Prophecy?" Lucinda asked.

"Who told you about that?" Greg asked.

"No, I just overheard some people talking about it on the street, and I felt I should ask you, so hoping you can tell me more about it," Lucinda asked.

"Why do I feel you're lying?" Greg said.

"I'm not lying, Grandpa. I'm telling you the truth," Lucinda replied.

"The Book of Prophecy is said to contain prophecies and findings on things we don't think exist in this world. It is one of the most powerful and dangerous books ever.

My father told me that the one who was once in possession of the book used it for evil. According to him, the book had always been kept in an ancient temple, and the only one who could read and understand the writings in the book was the priest of the temple, who changed from being good; and started using it for evil.

And one day, while amid prayers, the book closed by itself, and every effort was made to open it, but it proved abortive. It was left there and forgotten. Shortly after that, the priest died, and a few weeks after he was buried, the Book of Prophecy got missing.

No one cared to look for it because it was locked, and no one could understand the writings, and since then, history has forgotten about it.

So, can you see why I'm surprised that you are even asking me about it?" Greg said.

"But Grandpa, how can one find the book? Surely, it must be somewhere." Lucinda asked.

"You can never find the Book of Prophecy. It's not possible. It went missing from the mortal's eyes years back. My father used to say that the one who holds the key to unlock that book hasn't been born and when she is born, the book will find its way to her." Greg replied.

"It means the one who holds the key is a woman and that's she?" Lucinda contemplated on that for a while before continuing, "How did your father know, it will be a girl?

"That I didn't ask him. Maybe if he appears here now, you can ask him." Greg said and laughing as Lucinda joined in the laughter.

"Alright, Grandpa, I will be in my room," Lucinda said as she stood up and walked into her room.

She lay on the bed as she stared at the ceiling, contemplating on too many things that surrounded her life. Suddenly, she started soliloquizing.

"Book of Prophecy! Where will I find this book? Amber said the answers I seek are closer to me and that the answers are in the Book of Prophecy and now Grandpa is saying that the book can't be found. What will I do now? I'm so confused.

I just want my mom and dad free and for Star to vanish from the surface of this Earth and even in the world beyond. I want her case to be a closed chapter forever. Where do I find answers?

Where do I find that book? I need to place my hand on that book, else I might never hear from my parents again. Anya, where are you? Please come back if you can hear me; I need you right now.

I don't think I can do this on my own. I don't think I can win this. I'm confused. The road is getting darker, and I need a little ray of light. I don't want to give up, but I don't know if I can continue.

My strength is failing me. My parents' souls are engaged right now, and I need to set them free. Why is life so unfair to me? If I'm the one to unlock this book, I need it to come to me right now." Lucinda said as tears trickled down her cheeks.

"Wake up, dear," Maya said, tapping Lucinda. She had slept off while thinking about the current travail of her parents caused by Star.

"What's the time, Granny?" Lucinda asked.

"It's 5 pm. You need to wake up so you can also sleep at night." Maya said and left the room.

Lucinda did as she said and stood up, stretched her clothes before leaving the room. She went through the back door to get to the garden. She ran her hands through her hair as she thought about her mom and dad as she sat there.

"I miss you, Mom and Dad. I know you both can hear me even though you can't talk to me. Grandpa and Amber's exact words were life to me; that everything I've lost shall be returned.

I believe that. I know somehow you two are going to come back to me." Lucinda said. After muttering these words, she glanced at the building where Star said she lived; and had an inexplicable urge to search it out.

Lucinda got up and started towards the building. She got to the back door and pushed the door open, and it opened.

"There is no harm checking to see what's in this building that had been locked for years now," Lucinda said as she walked into the apartment.

Everywhere was dark, as Lucinda could barely see a thing. Finally, she saw a bookshelf standing at the corner of the parlor, and she checked it out. As she walked closer to it, Lucinda turned immediately when she heard a noise, only to see it came from rats. She had stiffened a bit.

"The books here are much," Lucinda said as she ran her hands over the book.

Suddenly she heard her name from a distance; and knew it was her grandmother calling. She quickly hurried out of the apartment as she closed the door behind her, sneaking back into the garden and sitting down as she shouted, "Grandma, I'm here."

"Where have you been? I have been looking for you. Dinner is ready." Maya said as she entered the garden to find Lucinda sitting down on the stone chair.

"Alright, Grandma," Lucinda said as she stood up and followed her grandmother inside. Her food was already on the table as she took the plate of food and sat close to her grandpa.

"Lucinda was asking me about the Book of Prophecy." Greg began breaking the silence.

"Where did you hear that from?" Maya asked.

"Someone was talking about it, so I asked Grandpa about it, but by the way, do you know where the book can be found?" Lucinda asked.

"You can never find that book; that's the truth. People have long forgotten it." Maya replied.

"So, there is no way I can get hold of it?" Lucinda asked.

"Even if you get hold of it, there is no way you can understand the language; the language is from the world beyond, and I don't think the girl who is said to have the key to open the book is even here on Earth yet. But, perhaps, she is here, and perhaps she isn't here, either." Maya replied.

"That's saddening," Lucinda replied.

"Or is there anything you're not telling us?" Maya chipped in, eyeing Lucinda from the corner of her eyes.

"That's true. Lucinda!" Greg said, also eyeing Lucinda at the same time.

"It's nothing. It's just that I wanted to know more about the book, and maybe I can even read it, but since you said I couldn't read it, and then let it be. I only overheard some people talking about it; that's all." Lucinda replied.

"It's okay. No problem." Greg replied as they all ate their food silently.

Lucinda took the plates into the kitchen immediately after they were done and washed them up. Her grandparents were sitting down and discussing when she bade them goodnight and walked into her room.

Once inside her room, she walked straight to her window and popped out her head, staring up at the sky above. But unfortunately, there was no single star in sight, and the Moon was half full.

"Don't you want to release me so I can set your parents free? I know you miss them. I can tell you how to free my body." It was Star speaking behind Lucinda, standing there gesticulating with her hands.

"You made the worst mistake of your life when you picked my parents as baits to get to me. I'm sorry, but you just picked a fight that is bigger than you; and just for the records, I will never set you free.

You can meet someone else to do that. Oh, now I remember, no one can set you free except me; you need me. I'm asking you nicely, free my parents else when the time comes. I won't hesitate to erase your entire existence from the surface of this Earth and even in the world beyond.

Please don't push me too far, Star. I have limits to which I can endure things. You wouldn't like me when I'm angry." Lucinda said as Star vanished immediately, an action that made Lucinda even more bent on finding the absolute truth about Star; and why she had to be the one to set her free.

She felt deep inside her that the answers she was looking for were right there in that house. She was determined to back and search around, hoping to lay her hands on something that could explain who Star was, and with that, she knew she would try to find out how to erase her chapter forever from existence. After staying for some more minutes, she went to her bed, lay down, and covered herself after Star had vanished.

"Getting to know how to get rid of you might take months; it might take years, but one thing is certain, once I get to find out, I'm getting rid of you, and I'm bringing my parents back. You know what will hurt me so much, and that's why you went for my parents. But, Star, you're going to lose this battle." Lucinda muttered as she closed her eyes and drifted off to bed.

LUCINDA HAD WOKEN UP

Chapter Four

Lucinda had woken up around 5 am as she slowly tiptoed out of her room with the lantern in her hand. At night, she couldn't sleep. She was disturbed that the Book of Prophecy could be in that house. She had this eerie, though inexplicable, feeling that she was right about this.

As she picked up her lantern, she went towards the back door and gently opened up the door. Walking outside, she was determined to see what was inside the house.

She walked towards the back door, pushed it open, and walked inside. She lifted the lantern high so she could see. The whole building was covered in dust and cobwebs, just as it was the first time she came. She didn't waste time, but went straight to the bookshelf to see if she could find anything relating to Star. She instantly picked up a book that looked strange. On the book's cover was inscribed "The Prophecy." Lucinda gasped at picking the book.

Her heart palpitated and raced swiftly. Could this be the book? She wondered. She knew her grandpa said the book had been missing for years; so obviously, there was no way this book could be here.

So, she thought as she took out the book from the shelf. Apart from the words" The Prophecy," the cover also had the symbol of the Moon and Stars on it. When Lucinda tried opening the book, it wouldn't open. Then she realized the book was the original Book of Prophecy that had been missing, according to her grandpa.

Lucinda held the book in one hand as she sneaked out of the apartment and went straight to her home. She crept inside and went to her room. Luckily, her grandparents weren't up yet.

Lucinda placed the book on her bed as she brought out a piece of cloth and wiped the dusty cover clean.

"How do I unlock this book because I need to know what's inside?" Lucinda muttered, after which she bent down as she took out the box she had hidden under her bed that contained the necklace. She opened it and took out her necklace. Then, raising it, she stared at the symbol on the Book of Prophesy.

"This is same symbol and size. This book is indeed the book that has been missing for years." Lucinda assured herself. She thought of placing the necklace close to the symbols on the book cover.

Lucinda hesitated for some seconds before going ahead with her intuition. She noticed a strange sound before the book suddenly unlocked as she did that. Lucinda smiled, nodded her head gently with a glee.

"So, my necklace is the key to unlocking this book? Woo. Wonderful! Now is the time to read." Lucinda said as she stood up and quickly locked her room. She placed the necklace back inside the box as she hid it and sat up properly before opening the Book of Prophecy.

Flipping through the pages of the book, she saw a drawing of a monstrous beast, the "Deadliest Star."

The letterings were strange, but it baffled Lucinda that she could still read and understand it. After observing the image for a split second, she turned to the next page, knowing that the beast's description would be there.

"Deadliest Star might appear as a pretty young girl to deceive and kill as many as she wants. But unfortunately, she is just the deadly monster whose image is on the first page, the demon that can't be killed so easily.

Star has lived for centuries but was sent into hibernation by the first daughter of the Moon and the Stars. Her spirit wanders about, but her body has been trapped and hibernated.

The only one who can set Star free is Lucinda, the third daughter of the Moon and the Stars. Star's spirit will come for Lucinda when she is of age to deceive her into freeing her body. Lucinda has five lives, but Star would come during her second life.

For Star to bring doom and chaos to the world, she must feast on the blood of the one who owns the magic seashell, Lucinda, daughter of Ann and Phil. If Lucinda ever releases Star, Lucinda must die, and sadly she won't come back to life the third time because Star will make sure it doesn't happen." Lucinda paused momentarily.

Her entire life had been written in a book, including the names of her parents, even before they were born. Beads of sweat appeared on her brows.

"I'm Lucinda, and this is my second life. So, I have three more lives. Hmmm, now I remember. The girl who looked like me told me not to make my powers visible to human eyes.

That was during my first life, and that is why Amber said on the night of the full Moon, Grandpa didn't notice that one Star was missing, and now it's just three, which means three more lives are left." Lucinda thought silently, nodded continuously for some seconds before continuing.

"So, Star is a demon. It's not just about releasing my grandparents. She would come for me because, for her to achieve her aim, she had to feast on my blood. I am the one in possession of the seashell. Wow! Things are making sense now." Lucinda said as she closed the book.

"This is the book that has been missing for years, and I'm the girl child that Prophecy said will be the one to unlock it. That girl child is me.

My mom gave birth to Lucinda, but she doesn't know she gave birth to another human being. She brought a queen to this Earth. If I don't release Star, I will never hear from my parents, and if I release her, I will have to die. This is tricky. What do I do now? Something has to be done." Lucinda said as she stood up and opened her windows as a glimmer of the sunray came right in.

Lucinda hid the book where her grandparents wouldn't find it as she left the house. She was going to the oak tree. Lucinda couldn't wait. Some questions needed to be answered. Maybe Amber might have the answers to those questions.

Lucinda was surprised to see Amber resting her head on the oak tree. She was waiting for her.

"When did you get here?" Lucinda asked immediately. She got closer to Amber.

"I knew you were going to find the book, and I knew you would come to meet me this morning to ask questions," Amber replied.

"Star is a demon." Lucinda burst out.

"I know," Amber said.

"You knew all about this, and you never told me?" Lucinda asked.

"I told what I knew. Even if I had told you, there are still things I wouldn't have said because I don't know them. I told you all the answers you seek are in that book, including everything about yourself." Amber replied.

"I can't be free Star. She would come for my blood because I have the Seashell, but I need to know how to free my parents, and I need to know how to end and erase Star forever from existence." Lucinda said.

"You only read the first page about Star, and you're already here to ask me questions? Patience! Patience! Why don't you read more and try to find out things yourself?" Amber replied, but Lucinda thought otherwise.

"It is called the "Book of Prophecy," so it contains prophecies of what will happen in years. But it doesn't contain solutions on how to go about the problem. So, I need your help, Amber. I need to know what to do to stop all this." Lucinda pleaded.

"I'm only a seer, and I can only offer solutions when I know the solutions to the problem, but in this case, it is only the book and her that can help you," Amber replied.

"Who is her? Who are you referring to? What's her name, and where can I find her?" Lucinda asked.

"You're just funny. You can't find her. She will come when you need her, but now I don't think you need her. That's why she isn't here yet." Amber replied.

"But you know I need her now. I need to talk to her, whoever she is, so long she has the answers to my questions. I need answers to this predicament. I need to know how to free my parents first." Lucinda replied.

"When you have read the important prophecies about yourself, then she will come. But, for now, you need to go back home and read everything. And put your necklace away, but your bracelet is still on your wrist." So, Amber observed as she looked quizzically at Lucinda.

"The bracelet is from my grandmother; I can't remove it. She is just like my mother, and as for the necklace, it's a gift from Anya. Unfortunately, she is not here, so what's the need to put it on when the person who gave it to me has been away for about a year now? The necklace reminds me so much about Anya. So, I had to put it away, and yes, it was the necklace that unlocked the book." Lucinda replied, sighing.

"Put the necklace back for your safety. You need it now. I might be a seer, but I can't understand the writings in that book. You're the only one who can understand the writing. You're the girl child the world has been waiting for. You need to go back home. Your grandparents will be awake any moment now. The journey has just started." Amber said as she stood up and walked away.

"And she didn't tell me about the one that needs to help me. Amber is so strange. I wonder if her grandmother knows the girl she is living with isn't a child, but a grown-up stuck in the body of a child." Lucinda said as she sighed and walked away.

Lucinda got home and sneaked back into her room. Her eyes were already getting weak. She knew she had to sleep, as she didn't sleep throughout the night. By the time she woke up, it was already noon. She quickly stood up as she hurriedly had her bath, after which she dressed up and went to the sitting room to see her grandparents.

"You didn't wake me up?" Lucinda asked, looking at her grandmother.

"Yea, because I didn't want to disturb you, as I felt you slept late yesterday," Maya replied.

"Well, she came into the room to check if you're still breathing." Greg offered.

"Your food is in the kitchen," Maya said as Lucinda smiled and walked to the kitchen to pick up her food. She then walked back to her room and locked the door behind her. Lucinda placed the food on her bed. Next, she took out the Book of Prophecy.

She flipped through the pages as she came across the word: **"ERASED FROM THE WORLD BEYOND."** And she started reading as her heart raced.

"For years, questions were being asked on how to erase Star from the world beyond, but the only one who has such powers is yet to be born. Her name is Lucinda, and she knows the trick on how to erase Star from this world. For the daughter of the Moon and the Stars to erase Star from this world, she will need the beast's help, three in one.

Star is a demon who must be erased by all means because if Star eventually wakes from hibernation, it means doom for the whole world."

"I still don't get it. Three in one beast? Why is this getting more complicated?" Lucinda asked, turning the pages of the book.

"Bring back the beast, and then you will find the key to how to destroy Star. Her presence is needed in the ritual."

After reading this, Lucinda kept flipping through the book's pages, but it was all blank. No, no, no." Lucinda cried, almost at the brink of tears. She became frustrated.

"This can't be happening. Why are the remaining pages blank? I still need answers. How do I free my parents? That's the most important thing to me right now." Lucinda cried as she ran her hands on her hair and sighed. Since she knew she couldn't do anything else about it, Lucinda hid the book back as she gobbled her food.

When she was through, she took the plate and went straight to the kitchen, washed it, and placed it correctly on the rack before walking to the exit door.

"Where are you going?" Greg, who was seated on the couch, asked.

"I need to see someone; I'll explain when I get back," Lucinda said as she fled the house.

She went straight to the oak tree and was surprised to see Amber waiting for her. She sat on the ground with her back against the tree trunk.

"The book didn't tell me how to free my parents, and the remaining pages of the book are blank. I need answers, please. Setting my parents free is the most important thing to me right now. Nothing else matters to me at this moment." Lucinda said as soon as she sat down.

"The book has already covered the message you need to know for now. It is a book that opens to you as you need to know. It is left to you to bring back the three-in-one beast. Perhaps once her presence is sensed, the rituals on how to erase Star will be revealed in the book." Amber replied.

"And that's another thing I don't understand. Who is this three-in-one beast? Who is he or who is she? This isn't fair, from one thing to the other. As much as I want to erase Star from this world, I also need to set my parents free. They have done nothing to deserve to be caged by Star. I need to hear their voice even if I can't be able to see them again." Lucinda said.

"You're so quick to forget; you can't tell me you do not know the three-in- one beast. You have met her, and you still have to bring her back to reveal the rituals to you. I believe after the ritual is done, your parents will be free, and you will hear from them again. But for now, bring back the beast." Amber said.

I have met no three-in-one beast, and I don't know how to bring anyone. This task is tiring. I'm getting tired and fed up. Why does everything around me revolve around complex tasks? Why do I live my life in perpetual pain and agony? Why do I have to go through so much stress in doing something that would benefit the whole world? Lucinda said.

"Do you want to free Star? If Star ever wakes up from hibernation, the whole world is in ruin. Perhaps it's time for you to ask your grandparents questions about the demon that once terrorized this world, the demon that had the mark of a Star on her. You can ask them. The beast's presence must be felt for the rituals to be revealed to you. So, bring her back, Lucinda, and stop whining. You're not a baby anymore. If you're the daughter of the Moon and the Stars, then act like one and stop whining like a child," Amber said as she turned and walked out on Lucinda.

"It is obvious she is angry," Lucinda muttered, and trudged back home.

"Your time is ticking; when will you set me free?" It was Star's voice, with a bit of tease in her tone. Lucinda knew it was Star, so she didn't bother looking back.

"And what makes you think I will free you?" Lucinda replied.

"I have your parents under chains. I can hurt them if I have to. I'm already running out of patience; free me!" Star bellowed.

"I doubt if you can even hurt a fly. I'm pretty sure that the only power left in your system was what you used to stop my parents' voice from reaching to me. You have no powers left. Your body is still in hibernation, so you can virtually do nothing. Only when you're free from hibernation, can you talk about hurting people, but for now, you're powerless. You need me to free you and my blood so you can continue existing. So, listen, you don't have to threaten me with hurting my parents because I know you can't!" Lucinda shrilled.

For a second, Star was taken aback on hearing these words, but she suddenly exclaimed, "Whatever you're planning you will fail. I'm promising you that. You can't erase me from this world." Star said, indignant.

"I hope you know the power to erase you from this world lies in my very hands. So, don't try my patience, Star. Don't push me to the wall because I promise I'll make life unbearable for you before I annihilate you, and let me warn you, don't you ever appear in my path to tell me anything about releasing you. Your case is a closed chapter.

You have terrorized the world enough. The first Lucinda could put you into hibernation; the second Lucinda, which is me, will erase you from this world and the world beyond." Lucinda replied as she watched Star disappear right in her front, with a hissing sound.

"Imagine the guts," Lucinda said as she sighed and continued walking home. She stepped inside, and her grandpa was sitting on the rocking chair, relaxing.

"You're back," Greg remarked as soon as Lucinda sat down close to him.

"Tell me about the demon that terrorized the world years ago, the demon with the mark of a Star on her body." Lucinda fired at Greg as soon as she sat down.

"Who told you that, Lucinda, because I'm sure you didn't hear it from the mouth of the passersby?" Greg asked, with eyes popping out in surprise.

"I was lucky to meet Amber, the seer. She told me about it. She said she would meet you when the time was right. Amber is back again, and it takes only the special ones to know she is the seer who lived years back then. Amber died and reincarnated back to life. She is on a mission close to finding that which had made her kept coming back to Earth." Lucinda replied.

Greg dropped in his hand when he heard what Lucinda said before asking her: "What did you just say?"

"Lucinda ..." Greg shrieked and was about to say more before Lucinda gently cut him off.

"Grandpa, please just tell me about the demon. I need to know. Don't start thinking that I'm going crazy again, please." Lucinda said. Greg considered her words, mopped at her one more time before deciding to let her know what he knew.

"I was little then, but I knew what was happening around us. The demon was called Star because she had the mark of a Star on her body. She killed many. The property was lost. People lived in fear. Everyone was scared. I never got to see her because my parents ensured I was inside.

She was close to destroying this world when she engaged in a fierce battle with a young lady. The young lady looked like a normal mortal, but possessed strong magical powers. Her name was Lucinda. She could defeat the demon, which she later placed into hibernation, which is more like a sleeping spell, after which Star's body disappeared.

According to Lucinda, it's actually in a place where humans can't set their eyes on her. When Lucinda questioned why she didn't kill Star the demon, she replied that the one who holds the power to kill Star was yet to be born. That's the little I know, and until today no one has seen the body of Star, and history is slowly forgetting about her." Greg replied.

"Interesting," Lucinda replied.

"Don't say interesting because if you were alive during that time, you wouldn't have survived it. Now tell me where you saw Amber, the seer." Greg asked, still wide-eyed.

"She came to me because I'm special. She said I'm the daughter of the Moon and the Stars. She also said the exact words you used, that light is coming to bring back everything it took from me." Lucinda replied.

"Then why can't I see her?" Greg said

"When the time is right, you will. I know you believe me." Lucinda said.

"Of course; I believe in you. No one knows the story behind your birth, so if she called you the daughter of the Moon and the Stars, then she is aware of the wish your mom made before giving birth to you." Greg said.

"Thanks, Grandpa. I will be in my room now." Lucinda said as she stood up and walked into her room.

"So, this is true. It happened in this world. Star is indeed a demon who has been in hibernation for years, and the day she is free, she will feast on the blood of the one who owns the Seashell, which was why she wanted to make me her friend. She wanted to manipulate me into setting her free. And when that wasn't possible, she picked my parents. It's been a whole six months, yet I haven't heard from my parents. I swear, Star, you will pay dearly for this," Lucinda said as she lay on the bed.

"How do I go about in finding the three-in-one beast? Amber said I had seen her before, but I'm certain I haven't seen her. Can't she be wrong then? Why is this happening? Why does everything have to be in riddles and puzzles?

Why can't they tell me things in a simplified form?" Lucinda muttered and sighed as she lay on her bed. Next, she took out the box containing the necklace, opened it, and placed it on the bed. She hid the box back under her bed after bringing out the necklace.

She held the necklace as Anya's memories flooded her mind. "Why can't you just come back and save me from all this pain and trouble? I need you. You said you were going to come back when I needed you. Isn't it obvious that I need you now? Can't you sense it, Anya?

This young girl here needs you. Even if I have done nothing wrong to make you leave for this long, I'm sorry. I miss you, and I miss my parents, too. You're the only one who I can talk to now. Please come back. I can't keep wearing this necklace when the soul that gave me the necklace is nowhere to be found. Anya, come back, please. The day is getting darker already, and I need you. I want you back.

I am the daughter of the Moon and the Stars, pleading; and begging that you come back home." Lucinda said as her tears dropped on the necklace. She then wore the necklace back on her neck. She closed her eyes and drifted off to sleep.

"Wake up, Lucinda; it's already late. Come and eat dinner." Maya said, tapping Lucinda, who slowly opened her eyes.

"Is it night already?" Lucinda asked, wiping her eyes.

"Yes, and you need to come and eat," Maya said and left the room immediately. Lucinda sat up and followed suit. She ate her dinner in silence as she thought of what to do that night.

But one thing was sure to her: either Anya came back to her that night, or she would never care anymore about all these. She had waited for a very long time.

"Lucinda, what's the problem? It seems your mind is somewhere else?" Greg asked.

"Don't worry about it, Grandpa. I'm fine." Lucinda replied.

"Are you sure, or you don't want to share with us? You have been picking on your food, which shows something is wrong," Maya said.

"I'm fine. Never mind." Lucinda said as she hurriedly finished her food to avoid her grandparents throwing more questions at her. She took her plates to the kitchen and washed them all when she was done.

"Goodnight. I'm off to bed." Lucinda said as she walked past her grandparents.

"The necklace; you put it back on." Greg asked as Lucinda stopped and answered, "I needed closure, so I wore the necklace.

Lucinda hurriedly walked into her room. She brought out the Book of Prophecy and placed it on her bed. She was tired of doing it all alone. To her, Anya had to come back. After all, she promised she would come back when she needed her.

For a year and a few months now, Lucinda had waited for her, but today she would call her out wherever she was. She made a promise to her, and so she had to keep her promise. Lucinda swore to make sure Anya would hold to that promise by coming back to her that night.

WHEN LUCINDA WAS SURE THAT EVERYONE WAS ASLEEP

CHAPTER FIVE

When Lucinda was sure that everyone was asleep, she locked her doors and clung to the Book of Prophecy while touching her necklace and closing her eyes. Then, after meditating for some minutes, she opened her eyes to see herself at the bush path where she usually meets with Anya. She sat on the ground and placed the book on her lap as she ran her fingers through her hair.

When I was trying to heal from Anya's sudden departure, Star came in, only to cage my parents' spirit shortly after. It's been months now since I heard from my parents. It feels like the whole world is against me. I don't just know what to do anymore. Life has been terrible. As much as I want to hear the voice of my parents again, my life is also on the line. Millions of souls will be lost if Star comes back as she wishes. So again, I don't just know what to do. How do I continue living every day without hearing from my parents? I'm used to hearing their voices from the beyond; I'm used to hearing their voices every day, though I can't see them. They have become my addiction, and I want to set them free, but if I yield to Star's request, then millions of lives and my own life will be at stake as well." Lucinda muttered so long that she started weeping, and then quakes of sobs set in eventually as she continued soliloquizing.

"Anya, I need you to come home. It was here that you promised me you would come back whenever I needed you. I need you now, Anya. The whole world is crumbling at my feet.

I need to do something before everyone gets hurt. I've hurt already. Star has caged my parents' souls. And somehow, I got this Book of Prophecy, and I've been told before I can do anything that the three-in-one beast has to be around before the next step starts on how to destroy Star begins. Anya, I'm suffering; life has been way too harsh for me.

I have tried and tried, but new problems come up every morning. This isn't what I'm expected to go through as the daughter of the Moon and the Stars. I can't do this on my own anymore. Anya, I need you back. Just come home. This is your home, too. My home is your home; my birthplace is your home. I'm pleading with you, Anya.

I need you now; else, I might go insane." Lucinda shouted as her voice echoed, and tears trickled down her cheeks, dripping down on the Book of the Prophecy in her hands.

Lucinda was tired. As much as she wanted to erase Star forever from existence, she still needed her parents back. She was in a dilemma. She was unsure what the three-in-one beast was and where to find it. She was unaware of how she could handle the situation, where to start, and how.

To make it worse, she was on her own, with no one to help at the moment. She knew she was getting fed up with everything. She was immured that it suddenly ceased after she started hearing her parents' voices.

All she craved for was a stress-free life where she could get to listen to her parents' voices every day, interact with them, laugh with them, but sadly those were mere wishes, a mirage.

She sat there on the ground, so sad that she didn't know when it was midnight. Then, just as it was midnight, the howls of the wolves could be heard in the forest from a distance. Lucinda paid little attention as she lay on the floral ground, crying. She was on the verge of giving up.

Lucinda hurriedly stood up and heard some movements behind her, a bit frightened. Then, clutching tightly to the Book of Prophecies in her hands, she turned to look as she beheld what she had been hoping to see these past months.

"Anya!" Lucinda shouted as she ran and hugged Anya tightly.

"I'm back, and I'm never leaving again. This is my home now. You have made your place of abode my home, and I can't disobey your orders." Anya whispered into Lucinda's ears as they hugged each other.

"Is it a promise that you're not going back again?"

"Yea, it is. Sure." Anya assured.

"I have missed you, Anya," Lucinda said as Anya slowly wiped off the tears welling in Lucinda's eyes.

"Stop crying, my dear queen. I stay; I'm not leaving you ever again. This is my home now." Anya reassured, smiling.

"Anya, I'm confused. Life has never been the same since you left. You left, and everything went with you. I got to meet this girl Star, and later on, I realized she was just a demon who wanted me to free her in exchange for my parents' souls.

She caged my parents' voices so they wouldn't communicate with me. She asked me to free her if I ever wanted to hear from my parents again. But I can't. Star is a demon, and if she is eventually freed, she is coming for me because she needs the blood of the one who has the magic Seashell before she can bring total ruin and destruction to this world.

This Book of Prophecy hasn't given me a clue on how to deal with Star and free my parents at the same time. Amber said the spirit of the three-in- one beast has to be felt before being told what next to do.

I'm confused, Anya. I don't know who the three-in-one beast is or where or how to find it. I need to set my parents free. Life took them away from me at a very tender age, and the only thing I console myself with is the fact that I can hear their voices, but suddenly Star appeared on the scene and put a stop to that. I can't hear them anymore. Star is still asking that I free her, but this book here won't say anything about destroying her. I'm losing it, and right now, I need help before making any mistakes.

Anya, I need to hear my parents' voice, or else I might hurt myself. I might inflict an everlasting injury on myself. The thought of not hearing their voice is driving me insane. Please help me, Anya.

I need my parents back. I need to hear their voices again, please." Lucinda pleaded as she burst out crying again.

"Calm down; just calm down. The three-in-one beast is me. I'm the beast whose presence needs to be felt before the next clue can be given to you. How did you forget so soon?" Anya asked.

Lucinda trembled on hearing that. Everything just flooded back to her memory. How could she have forgotten so soon? She wondered. She scratched her head before saying, "Maybe I have gotten used to your beautiful human face. I forgot that the first day you approached me here, you were three-in-one."

"Well, I'm here now," Anya replied.

"What took you so long, Anya? You didn't want to come back.

"That's because you never needed me. You just wanted closeness with me and a friend with whom you can relate. The day you needed me was today when you called and asked me to make your home my home, too. That was when you needed me back." Anya replied.

"So, all this while you heard me, but you only came back because I asked you to make this place your home, too? Hmmm. Interesting." Lucinda muttered.

"A visitor will always go home. But when she moves into the house, you will have every opportunity to see her." Anya replied.

"Okay. I got it. So now that you are here, tell me how I can free my parents; I need to free them. Star has kept them hostage for so long. They don't deserve this." Lucinda said.

"They deserve it. Why can't you just free me? Do you have to invite Anya over to this place? I thought she was gone for good? It was Star's authoritative voice that sounded nearby.

Without warning, Lucinda saw Anya turn into a three-in-one beast. Lucinda watched in awe. She hadn't seen Anya transform into a werewolf before. The words about her were right, indeed. Anya was a deadly beast. When Lucinda saw Anya was about to charge towards Star, she called out her name.

"Anya, she isn't worth it. She is just a spirit, remember. She is so powerless. She still needs me to free her body before she can do anything to this." Lucinda shouted as Anya cast a deadly look at her.

"I know you're angry, but trust me, she is not worth it. She is just here to make you angry. Please calm down, Anya, I beg of you. It's just a matter of days before I extirpate her totally from this world and in the world beyond. Her chapter is about to be closed forever. So don't worry about her." Lucinda pleaded.

"Why don't you want to hurt her? Why?" Anya growled.

"She is going to set me free. She has to set me free, or she will never hear from her parents again. But, Lucinda, you're running out of time. Free me now!" Star shouted as Lucinda cast a glance at her. On saying this, Star bent down as she winced in pain before disappearing from view.

"What did I do? Lucinda asked as she looked at her hands and watched Anya transform into the woman she was before.

"A three-in-one beast, a werewolf, and a shape-shifter. What else do I need to know about you?" Lucinda asked, looking askance at Anya.

"You already know everything," Anya replied.

"What happened a few minutes ago? It felt like I wasn't myself. The last thing I remember is Star wincing in pain as she disappeared." Lucinda wondered at Anya, expecting some explanations from her.

"You allowed your powers to take over you. You couldn't control yourself; that's what happened," Anya replied.

"But I thought...."

"Humans, spirits, and even vegetation; all can feel a taste of your powers; none is immune to it. You can bring unending pain to anyone. Star isn't excluded, even though she is a demon. You were angry when Star uttered those words. She commanded you without knowing you hate anyone commanding you. The person I saw a few minutes ago wasn't Lucinda. You allowed anger to control you; you need to learn to control yourself." Anya replied.

"I'm sorry," Lucinda replied after reflecting on Anya's words.

"You don't need to be sorry. You live in a world of humans. Control your anger or else you might hurt someone," Anya replied.

"Okay. I got it. About my parents: please Anya, do something." Lucinda pleaded.

"The Book of Prophecy wanted my presence to be felt before the clue on how to deal with Star is explained to you. So, recheck the book." Anya replied.

"It's empty. There is nothing anymore to read. The pages are blank." Lucinda replied without bothering to check.

"The Book of Prophecy can't stop halfway; check again, Lucinda. And about your parents, extirpate Star first, and then your parents will come back. And listen, you barely have enough time to do so. Star might be in hibernation, but her spirits are getting stronger. I could sense it when she came here.

She might be powerless now, but she shouldn't be alive during the next full Moon." Anya replied as she quickly changed to a wolf. Anya was ready to leave.

"Promise me you're going to come back anytime, any day, I need you," Lucinda said.

"This is my home. I'm not leaving without letting you know," Anya said as she raced into the woods.

Lucinda picked the Book of Prophecy lying on the ground as she touched her necklace and closed her eyes. On opening her eyes, she saw herself in her room. She placed the book on her bed as she lay down beside the book, staring at the ceiling before delving into her normal soliloquy.

"I hope I win this battle. I hope fate gives me the chance to hear your voice again. I miss you, Mom and Dad. I do, and I will do everything possible to hear your voice one last time." Lucinda said as she cleaned the tears from her eyes almost immediately before dozing off.

****

"Why did you have to bring Anya? Send her back to where she belongs. I'm warning you, Lucinda." Star shouted, but Lucinda wouldn't take any of that.

"She is my friend, and she has every right to stay here, unlike you, that has killed so many people. And what makes you think I will ever set you free? I dare not, Star and I won't. Your next target has always been me. I already know you need to feast on my blood as the one in possession of the seashell before you can bring total ruin and damnation to the world.

I keep telling you, Star, soon your case will be a closed chapter; and of course, your memory shall be no more, though a sad memory it has always been. I doubt history will ever remember you." Lucinda replied.

"You're making me angry. I will hurt your parents, and you won't do anything about it. The sooner you free me from this hibernation, the better for you. Don't think I'm powerless; I'm getting stronger, you know." Star said and grinned.

"Ha-ha-ha! Alright, I have heard you, but I dare you to hurt my parents, then I'll make your exit from this world the most painful. I dare you, Star, and now listen to me; I don't know how you did it, and I don't care to know.

All I want you to know is that I'm giving you forty-eight hours. If you're not destroyed within these forty-eight hours, know that I'm not the daughter of the Moon and the Stars.

I accommodated you and listened to you because I thought you wanted a friend, and in the end, you were only trying to trick me into setting a deceitful soul like you, free. Forty-eight hours, Star, just forty-eight; that's what you've got, and then I will wave my last goodbye to you." Lucinda replied and walked away.

Lucinda woke up only to discover she had been dreaming. She stood up and walked towards her window and opened it.

"Awe! It's morning already." Lucinda exclaimed as she sat down on her bed.

"So, she came to my dream to warn me? I can't believe this. You might get stronger, but definitely, you won't be able to hurt me because I'm sure sending you to the abyss or wherever you came out from. That's a promise. It would have been okay if you didn't have to drag my parents into this mess, but you did. You knew how much my parents mattered to me, yet you played this game using them as baits.

That was the worst mistake you made, and now you're threatening to hurt them. Before I destroy you, I will make you have a taste of your own medicine." Lucinda muttered as she sat there over the window, looking out into the compound, with her left hand on her chin. Shortly after, she went back to her bed to look at the Book of Prophecy.

She flipped through the pages and was surprised to see written on the pages she presumed blank: "Destroying Star the Demon."

"Summon her spirit, and the three-in-one beast will guide you on what next to do." Lucinda closed the book and became pensive.

"This makes little sense. How do I find where Star's body is being kept? This is going to be the toughest thing ever." Lucinda said as she stood up and left the room.

Lucinda walked into her grandparents' room to see they were still sleeping. She held her necklace as she cast a glance at her grandparents. Her eyes turned white before she released her grip on the necklace.

"I'm sorry I had to do this, Grandpa and Grandma. I'm sorry I had to cast this spell on you. I promise to wake you both up once I return. But for now, I just have to save humanity.

The night of the full Moon is in seven days, and I barely have enough time left. I don't even know how many days it's going to take me to find her body. It's all for our good." Lucinda said with tears in her eyes as she looked at her grandparents one more time before she left them and walked into her room.

Lucinda took the bag and stuffed a few of her clothes. She hung the bag on her back as she walked to the door. She opened the door to meet Amber and Anya standing right there.

"How did you both get to know where I'm living?" Lucinda asked.

"Isn't that a stupid question, queen? You have made the right decision. Let's get going. We are making use of your horse." Amber said as she turned and went towards the backyard.

"I can find you anywhere you are, so step outside. I need to cast a protection spell on your house because your grandparents are inside," Anya said as Lucinda locked the door and shifted from her path. Anya closed her eyes. As she rose up, she emitted a thick white net, which appeared and disappeared again.

"It's done," Anya said as she walked towards the backyard.

Lucinda followed suit. She climbed onto the white horse while Anya and Amber used the brown horse.

"How long will it take before we get there?" Lucinda asked.

"The question is whether we can find the body before the date of the full Moon," Amber replied.

"I just want to end all this and free my parents. She threatened me in my dream that she would hurt my parents. I told her forty-eight hours ago. But before then, I will make her feel double the pain I'm going through right now. No one dares me and goes scot-free. I have been pushed to the wall by Star. My soul is aching; my heart is in pain. Because of Star, I have cast a sleeping spell on my grandparents.

And now I'm going through the stress of finding her body. Lucinda is angry," Lucinda shouted as lightning struck, followed by a thunder strike.

Both Anya and Amber experienced some chills on their bodies before Anya waved her hand as a portal opened before them. They hit the horses as they advanced into the portal, and it closed immediately as they went inside it.

They came out in a different world. Lucinda was becoming impatient. She turned to Anya and Amber and exclaimed, "I need to find her body before the next forty-eight hours!"

"Yes, my queen," Anya and Amber said in unison, slightly bowing their heads.

WE'RE RUNNING OUT OF TIME

CHAPTER SIX

"We're running out of time. I hope we find the body soon. Amber, you're a seer; please, you should be able to tell us where exactly we can find Star's body." Lucinda pleaded.

You're right. That's why I'm here, and I'm taking you to where Star's body is laid. The distance to cover is much, but don't worry, in the next five hours, we will be there." Amber assured.

"What? five hours? Is that not too much?" Lucinda exclaimed, mouth agape.

"Do you want to go back?" Anya asked, eyeing Lucinda.

"No, we have come a long way for us to turn back; and aside from my parents, Star needs to be destroyed because her continuous existence is inimical to the world," Lucinda said.

"Good," Anya replied as they continued galloping, following Amber.

They got to the foot of a mountain when Amber came to a halt, and Anya and Lucinda following behind also stopped.

"Why are we stopping here?" Lucinda implored a bit.

"The rest of the journey will be done by foot; we have to keep the horses here," Amber said, without looking behind.

"Hmmm. Anna and Phil might get hurt; wild beasts might attack them, and if anything happens to them, my grandparents will be devastated." Lucinda said.

"Anna and Phil?" Anya asked, surprised.

"I'm referring to the horses." Lucinda offered.

Lucinda gave the horses the names when her parents' spirit lived inside the horses, the reason the horses held a special place in her heart.

"Don't worry, Lucinda. They won't get hurt. Anya is going to cast a protection spell around them. With that, they won't be able to run away; neither shall any harm come close to them." Amber replied.

"Alright, Anya does it so we can get going," Lucinda replied, a bit impatiently.

Amber drew a circle around the horses as Anya cast a spell on the line that Amber drew, with a mist enveloping the horse.

"We can now go," Anya said. So, they continued their journey into the thick of the forest that stretched before them. Before long, they were to enter inside a hole-like cave right inside the bowel of the mountain.

"This place is dark; how do we see what's on the inside and know where we are going?" Lucinda asked, a little impatiently.

"I think that is left for you to sort out. You have the power to do that." Anya replied.

Lucinda walked into the hole as Amber and Anya followed behind. Lucinda closed her eyes as a ball of fire appeared in her hand, but she screamed, and the fire went off.

"What happened?" Amber asked.

"The fire; it was hurting me." Lucinda shrieked.

"Be in charge of your powers. They are not meant to hurt you; they are meant to obey you. Try again." Anya said.

Lucinda closed her eyes and repeated the same process as a ball of fire appeared in her hand, this time without a single heat. Finally, she raised her consciousness above that of the fire; and became in control of it.

"Lead the way," Anya said to Amber as they walked deeper into the hole while the fire burning in Lucinda's hand lighted their path.

"My hands are hurting," Lucinda complained after some distance inside the cave.

"That's because you're not concentrating; your powers are meant to obey you. So always stay on top of your powers; always!" Anya enthused.

As they kept walking, Lucinda hit something with her leg. She bent down to know what it was. She saw a human skull, and on looking around still, she saw human skeletons scattered on the floor. She became apprehensive.

"What are all these?" She asked.

"It is a place where Star feasts on her victims. These are their skeletons. Her body is placed inside here because this is the only place suitable for her." Amber replied.

"What's wrong, Lucinda?" Anya asked as she noticed the tears in Lucinda's eyes.

"I can hear their screams. I can hear them calling out for vengeance. I can hear them crying out to be saved. They might be dead, but their spirit still litters around here, waiting to be freed. I want to go home. They want to be free. They don't belong here. They are crying; they want to go." Lucinda said as Anya walked closer to her and placed her hand on her shoulder.

"You will free them soon, but first thing first," Anya said, patting her on the shoulder.

"Let me go. Release me. I want to go home." The spirits kept wailing as Lucinda remained bent.

"They are in pain. They have been here for years. They want to go home. They are screaming; they are pleading." Lucinda said in tears.

"They are my captives. You do not have any right to set them free. Go back to your world, Lucinda! You're not welcome here. Go back home. This is where they belong, and just for the records, no one can set Star's captives free. Leave my territory, Lucinda. Leave before I hurt you." Star shouted as everyone looked around, but they didn't see her.

"Lucinda, let's go," Amber said as Anya helped Lucinda up. So they continued on their journey, ignoring Star's threat. Soon they came to a fountain when Amber informed them they were closer to the body.

"How come there is light here?" Lucinda asked.

"Her body was kept in a place where the water never runs dry. As for the light, the mystery behind it is yet to be unveiled," Amber replied.

"So, where is her body?" Lucinda asked.

"In the water," Amber said as she slowly removed her sandals, after which she walked into the water as Anya and Lucinda followed suit. They had formed a circle as Lucinda looked around and asked again, "Where is her body?"

"Patience, Lucinda, patience," Anya replied as she stretched forth her hands for Amber and Lucinda to hold. They clung to her as Anya chanted strange words when the rocks inside the water started rumbling.

Lucinda was surprised when she saw what was happening, and at that instance, the rocks opened to expose Star's body lying peacefully on the cluster of pebbles of stones. She looked nothing like what Lucinda had seen. Yet, the Star she was seeing right before her was a beauty to behold, perhaps more beautiful than the lilies of the valley.

"It's unbelievable for me seeing a Beautiful Evil", Lucinda asked as she ran her hands over Star's face.

"The stars are always beautiful. They glitter like diamonds, and everyone always looks forward to seeing them in the skies. Star might be so beautiful, but the truth remains that she is one of the deadliest beings that has ever lived, and she has to go." Anya replied.

"Her beauty is so deceptive; hope you aren't having a change of mind?" Amber asked.

"No, I'm not going back on my words.

"Now, you have to summon her spirit," Anya replied.

"How will I do that, and why do we even have to summon her spirit here?" Lucinda asked.

"We don't have time for questions, Lucinda. try to see how you can summon her spirit because if you don't, there is no way else you can destroy Star. Just focus and concentrate. I know you can do this. You were chosen to be the daughter of the Moon and the Stars for a reason. Lucinda, this is one time to show it. Just concentrate." Anya replied.

Lucinda walked closer to the body and placed her hands on it, closing her eyes in the process. Then suddenly, she started mumbling gibberish. Before long, a ball of fire struck her hand, prompting her to withdraw her hand from the body.

"Try again. Just concentrate and call her. She will answer you. Once her spirit is here, she can't leave anymore, and she will be vulnerable." Amber replied.

Lucinda repeated the quick process, but nothing happened. She tried and tried, but it felt Star wasn't ready to appear. But Lucinda wouldn't give up. She became agitated as she once again placed her hands on the body as she closed her eyes and summoned Star's spirit. This time around, her tears started welling in her eyes. Shortly after, they started dropping on Star's forehead, and just immediately, lightning struck, followed by a thunderstorm as Star appeared.

"Why have you chosen to do this?" Star abruptly asked as soon as she appeared.

"Perhaps I wouldn't have come for you if you had left my parents out of this, but by doing so, you misfired. You would have played your game and not involved them, and I wouldn't have been here today. Instead, you took my source of joy from me, and you lied about who you were. My parents have done nothing wrong. I'm asking you to set them free now." Lucinda bellowed her command.

"And why will I do that? You will still wipe me off from this world and the world beyond, nevertheless. So, what's the essence of setting them free? I will not lose at both ends; never! Star bemoaned.

"I'm still asking nicely; set them free, Star," Lucinda whispered.

"And I said no! Never!" Star shouted.

Lucinda didn't waste more time with words as she bent down and brought out a dagger she had hidden in her shoes. She raised it and sliced it into the lifeless body, and just immediately, Star started bleeding at the exact place where the dagger pierced.

"It's your hand. Next is your heart. Finally, will you set my parents free, or do you still want me to torture you the more?" Lucinda asked as she raged.

"Even if she goes, your parents will still be set free somehow. It's of no use giving her enough time to talk. End her miserable life here and now. She has wasted thousands of souls. She has taken many into captivity. And even with the souls she had feasted on, she wouldn't allow their spirit to rest.

She still kept them hostage. What other punishment does she deserve, if not both physical and soulish death? Star deserves to die. Stab her in the heart. Let's end it all." Amber bellowed.

"Just do it, Lucinda. Do it and set her victims free; your parents will find their way back to you somehow; just do it," Anya added.

"Are you going to listen to them? I thought we had been friends all this while? I only wanted to be free "

"Free, so you can feast on my blood because I'm the one in possession of the Seashell? Free so you can continue from where you stopped? Free so you can bring damnation and ruin to this world? Free so you can wipe out my entire existence? Why will I free you when you end up killing me just to achieve your aim of ruining humanity?" Lucinda shrieked.

"You put me into this; more reason, I will have to kill you first. You placed me in hibernation for years; you ruined all my plans. That's why I'm coming for you." Star replied.

Lucinda raised her dagger and pierced it into the heart of Star's body, but as she tried pulling it back, the blade remained stuck right there.

"You have done your worst, Lucinda. You might have ended my very own existence, but I promise I will come back to Earth or the world beyond; I will, Lucinda. It might take years, but I will come back." Star screamed as she winced in pain.

They all stood there watching as Star's body slowly faded into thin air, with no trace of existence. After some minutes of silence from the three spectators, Anya walked closer to Lucinda and said as she patted her on the shoulder: "You don't look happy; you have already done it. Never mind; she isn't coming back. They are just mere words meant to scare you."

"I'm not scared or worried about her threats. I'm just sad that after everything, I couldn't set my parents free, after all. I feel I have let them down. I'm not worthy of being called their daughter. Now that Star is no more, where are my parents?" Lucinda replied.

"That's not true; you're a true queen. You have saved millions, and the world will remain entirely grateful to you. And about your parents, they will find a way to come back to you; have it at the back of your mind." Amber said and made to leave.

"Where are you going?" Lucinda asked, surprised.

"Her journey is done here on Earth. She is going back home," Anya said.

"I don't understand. I know we are on Earth but in a different place, somewhere far away from home, but what do you mean her journey is made here on Earth? You don't think about your grandmother? Wouldn't she look for you? Amber, Return home with us, please." Lucinda was agitated to the point of distraught.

"Did you not read in the Book of Prophecy that after Star is destroyed, Amber will go back home to where she belongs? I have waited all these years to meet you, and I'm glad I did. I know you will miss me. I know you would visit the oak tree after I'm gone; hoping to see me, but it's of no use. I might be gone, but I'm still closer to you than you may think. Just call my name, and I will answer. Call me in times of distress, in times of happiness, and I would answer.

Talking about my grandma, she wouldn't know that I was gone. All the memories we both had have been wiped off her head, same with the people who had an encounter with me. So, it's just like I never existed to them. Just call my name whenever you need me, and I will answer you. Goodbye, Lucinda; goodbye, Anya." Amber said as she waved and slowly vanished before their eyes.

"This isn't fair; this isn't the life I want. I don't wish to repeat my past again. Why do people I love leave me when I'd gotten used to them? Why is that so? It's just a matter of time before you leave too, Anya. So why do you all keep leaving me? Why, why has life punished me this way? Why?" Lucinda shouted as she burst out crying.

"Lucinda, Amber isn't gone forever. She stayed this long to meet you and offer the help she is fated to offer you. And that she has done. So, she just has to return home. Amber had lived for many centuries." Anya said.

"I want to go home; take me home." Lucinda shrieked as she started walking out.

When they got to the spot where the bones were littered on the floor, Lucinda cast one glance at them before leaving, still feeling sad for them. Shortly after they got to the horses, they mounted and galloped away. Lucinda was in no mood to talk. She was just sad.

Soon after, they went to the portal that led to the visible world. "We're here. I'll open the portal, which will take us directly to your house." Anya said.

Lucinda kept mute as she wiped the tears that were threatening to fall off her eyes. She watched as Anya opened the portal, and there she was right in their backyard. She came down from the horses, same with Anya as she held them and led them inside the stable before locking them up.

"What's wrong, Lucinda? I can see you're not happy." Anya asked.

"Why should I be? I know, of course, it's just a matter of time before you tell me you're leaving, too. I think it's time I came to terms with it that everyone who comes into my life will leave when I least expected it. Thank you for helping me gets rid of Star.

Thank you, Anya. Perhaps I should just start getting used to how life is treating me. Somehow, someday, I will find a way to free my parents; and all those souls trapped in that cave calling out for help. Thank you, Anya. I need to wake my grandparents up." Lucinda said as she walked away, but Anya called her back.

"Lucinda, I know you're sad, but I'm not leaving. I know you're angry, but there are certain prices you have to pay for being the daughter of the Moon and the Stars. Not everyone will be with you forever.

You just have to get used to it and get ready because anyone might leave you. And today is Wednesday. We might have spent hours out there, but over here, we have spent days," Anya said.

"Thank you," Lucinda said as she walked into the house. She made straight to her room as she lay down and cried herself to stupor.

"What kind of miserable am I living? Why would I ask someone to come back, and then I will still have to lose another? Amber, why didn't you tell me you would leave me soon? You just kept mute and acted like everything was fine. And Now You're Gone. You came, and you stole my heart, and you left like the wind? Why is it so? Why is my life like this? Why does life keep bringing people to me when they know they won't stay? Why? What is wrong with me? I hate this. I simply do!"

Lucinda started crying as she lay on her bed. Finally, after some minutes of crying her heart out, she stood up and walked into her bathroom to take her bath. Lucinda came out, changed her clothes, and walked into her grandparents' room when she was done. She then tapped them, and they became awake.

"What are you doing here? Aren't you meant to be sleeping?" Maya said, stretching herself.

"It's already evening. Get up so you can prepare something for us to eat." Lucinda said.

Maya stood up as Lucinda hugged her and did the same to Greg.

"Okay, okay. Why are you hugging us tight like this? What's the problem?" Greg asked.

"I'm surprised." Maya replied.

"I just missed you both, and I don't want any of you to leave me. I won't be able to survive it if any if you should leave me." Lucinda said.

"We're not leaving you; we're going to stay here with you, okay?" Greg said.

"Thanks, Grandpa," Lucinda said as she walked out of the room.

"Strange. Something is amiss." Maya said as she left the room to prepare something for dinner. What they didn't know was that they had been asleep for days now.

Lucinda left the house as she trekked down to the oak tree. She sat on the branches as she looked around, and tears fell off her eyes.

"I will never see you again, right?" Lucinda said, picking a dead leaf from the ground.

"You were with me all these whiles, and you said nothing about leaving, but it was after everything that you told me you were leaving. That's not fair, Amber. I have wanted my grandpa to meet you, but now he can't. I wish you had stayed longer, Amber. I wish you could hear me and please come back home." Lucinda said as she wiped the tears from her eyes.

"You know things aren't always what they seem. We don't always get what we want. The more reason you should treasure every second you get to spend with someone." A voice sounded next to Lucinda as she looked up to see Amber.

"Amber, you're back! Lucinda exclaimed, standing up.

"You're funny. I didn't leave you for once. I never left you, and I wouldn't leave you. I'm always with you. Just call my name, and I will be there. You will always be the daughter of the Moon and the Stars, and there is no way I can leave you." Amber replied.

Lucinda touched Amber, but was shocked when she faded away.

"I wish this was real. You are gone, yet you said you're not gone. How come I can't even feel you? I need to touch you and hug you one last time." Lucinda replied.

"Call me whenever you need me, and I'll always be with you, even if you can't see me." The voice replied.

Lucinda wiped her tears as she journeyed back home. Lucinda was a few steps close to her house when she heard some voices inside the portal crying out to her, pleading that she free them so they could rest.

But she kept walking, and soon after, she got home, had her dinner, and retired to her room. She locked her room as she took out the Book of Prophecy, hoping to find a clue how to free those spirits and her parents.

She flipped through the pages, but nothing was there to grab. She then dropped the book and took out her seashell, rubbed her hands on it, and talked.

"I can't remember the last time I made a wish, but right now, I'm in pain, and I need your help. I might have destroyed Star, but the spirits of those she killed are waiting to be free so that they could find eternal rest. They are crying; they are pleading with me. They just want to be freed. I don't know how to go about it. I don't know how to set them free, but I need them to be free. They are wailing. Their tears are disturbing me. I can hear them; they just want to rest.

They have been in bondage for years. They just want to rest. Please free them; free all that Star has caged that they may find rest and reunite with members of their families who died before them.

Free them; I may live without hearing the wails of these innocents. Free them because they need to be freed. They are not supposed to be prisoners. Please stop their sadness and misery and free them." As soon as Lucinda stopped talking, she heard lightning, followed by the bellow of thundering.

"I believe you have granted my wishes," Lucinda said as she wiped her tears and put the seashell back to the box with the Book of Prophecy. She then lay on the bed, and soon she started hearing the voices of laughter. She smiled, convinced that those souls had been freed, just as she desired. Finally, she closed her eyes and drifted off to sleep.

****

"I want to see you; it's been months, Lucinda," Anna said

"Mom, how come you're here? What of Dad?" Lucinda asked.

"I'm here," Phil said.

"How you come? I thought Star caged you both? Why do I see you both instead of just hearing your voices?" Lucinda asked, pleasantly surprised.

"We want to see you." Anna and Phil said in unison as they both walked away while Lucinda kept calling them to come back. Shortly after, Lucinda woke up sweating, and it was then she knew it had been a dream. "What kind of dream is this?" She muttered.

"They both kept saying they wanted to see me, yet they were walking away from me. What does that mean? Well, I must find out somehow." She said, and she lay back on her bed and slept off.

Three months were already gone, yet Lucinda didn't meet with Anya. She had this icy feeling that she was gone, just like Amber. But she knew she wouldn't be able to hold on to the temptation of not meeting with Anya. Her soul was already knitted with Anya's.

On a specific night, when she was sure her grandparents were asleep, she locked her door and clung to her necklace; opening her eyes, she saw herself in the exact spot where she met with Anya. She cast a furtive glance around, hoping to see Anya, but she was nowhere to be found.

"Anya, where are you? I know I haven't come to see you for months now. I only felt dejected, since everyone I had ever loved left me. I felt maybe you would not stay too like the rest of them.

I was tired of bonding with people and having to lose them the next day. I was so tired. I knew you were going to go too, but today I felt unable to hold on not seeing you anymore. I know you can hear me where ever you are now. I just thought I should say hello again, and I miss you. I miss Amber, as well." Lucinda shouted into the space before her.

"When you said you wanted this place to be my home, I obeyed. This is my home, and I'm never leaving." Anya said, coming out from the bush.

When Lucinda saw the other three figures coming with her, she shifted slightly. Then, she snapped her hand, and the ball of fire appeared on her hand as she looked at the faces of the people coming with Anya and was surprised to see her parents.

She ran and hugged them, crying profusely in the process, totally short of words. She didn't know what to say. She was simply given to crying, as their appearance was unexpected to her. And finally, after a long time, Lucinda muttered, audible enough for her parents, "I missed you both." But she couldn't stop sobbing.

"We missed you too." Anna and Phil said.

"How did this happen? I thought Star caged you both? How come I can see you both in the flesh? How is that possible?" Lucinda asked while trying to wipe away her tears.

"Everything is possible because you're the daughter of the Moon and the Stars, though you are not aware of your powers. I didn't know who my child was until now." Anna said.

"We didn't know you have been conferred with so much power and ability to do things humans can't do," Phil said.

"We waited every night for you, but you weren't coming. Then, finally, Anya assured us you would come someday. After that, we never stopped hoping." Anna said.

"I had a dream about this. Now I understand it was a message." Lucinda said.

"Yes, it was, but you did not understand it. After you made the wish with the seashell, it granted more than you asked for. It freed not only your parents; it granted them the opportunity to spend time with you from 12 am till 3 am. They have waited for 90 days without seeing you, but I kept telling them that someday you would come out.

"Hey, wait a minute; I saw three people with you, Anya. Where is the third person?" Lucinda asked, looking around.

"I'm here," Amber said, revealing herself as Lucinda rushed and hugged her.

"Ha-ha-ha! Oh Amber! I missed you so much." Lucinda said.

"Awe same here. I haven't seen you in the oak tree for months. I would wait for you there in the morning, and I would be here at night. You took a long while to realize that we're never going to leave you; you're special." Amber said.

"Thank you, Anya, Amber, Mom and Dad, for never giving up on me. I promise to come to you every day." Lucinda replied, offering a huge smile.

They hugged each other as they all sat down on the floor and talked about everything that had happened. And while they were still talking, Lucinda watched as her parents and Amber faded into thin air. She was startled.

"They are coming back, right?" Lucinda asked Anya.

"Yes, sure, they are; it's already 3 am. You need to go back home now." Anya said, standing up.

"Anya, thank you so much. I hope one day I could make you live among humans, not in the forest." Lucinda said.

"Till then, Lucinda," Anya said as she turned into a wolf and disappeared into the forest.

Lucinda smiled as she closed her eyes, touching her necklace, and in no time, she appeared in her room. Shortly after, she lay back on her bed to sleep.

"Thank you for bringing my parents back to me. I have my Dad, Amber and Anya. What more do I need? I just want to live in peace forever. The daughter of the Moon and the Stars is saying thank you to the Supreme Being." Lucinda said as she smiled, and before she knew it, she was off to sleep.

THE END

ABOUT THE AUTHOR

Dennis WC Wong

Mr. Wong currently works at Kaiser Permanente in Oakland, CA as a Nurse Assistant in the Operating Room Department and became a Licensed Vocational Nurse doing home health care. It was only after exploring the paint sales industry that he felt drawn to pursue a career in healthcare. Backed by an Associate of Arts in Retail Marketing from Chabot College, Mr. Wong earned a Bachelor of Science in Business Management-Personnel and Industrial Relations from California State University, Hayward. He was presented with the Albert Nelson Marquis Lifetime Achievement Award by Marquis Who's Who in 2020. Also, as a Sterile Processing Technician, Mr. Wong volunteers with Surgical Missions to Guatemala and Ecuador. He also owns a 1969 Ford Falcon Futura Sport Coupe. It has won awards at a couple of car shows and was featured in a 2024 calendar. After retirement, he plans to travel and experience other cultures around the world.

The author started his journey in 2002 when he wrote "**My Journey**" while attending a certified nursing assistant class at San Jose Vocational Center. Mr. Wong wrote "**The Apricot Outlook of Katherine Koon Hung Wong**", a memoir of his mother in January 2018. It started out as a term paper in a psychology class in 2005 entitled "**Senior Biography of My Mom Aged 77**". *His mother's Chinese middle name means outlook apricot. Apricots represent female elegance and the large seed is ovoid shaped like the eyes of an Oriental beauty.*

Mr. Wong's third book "**The Power of Passion**" is a fictional story of love embedded in passion and empathy.

"**Over the Distant Mountain Ranges**" is a three - part series of transmigration. The second book, "**Beyond the Ranges**" continues the mysteries, mysticism, and the supernatural. The third book "**Anya**" is when Lucinda finally achieves inner peace.